HER NEW YEAR
BABY SECRET

HER NEW YEAR BABY SECRET

BY

JESSICA GILMORE

MILLS
BOON

First published in Great Britain 2016
By Mills & Boon, an imprint of HarperCollins*Publishers*
1 London Bridge Street, London, SE1 9GF

Large Print edition 2017

© 2016 Harlequin Books S.A.

Special thanks and acknowledgement are given to
Jessica Gilmore for her contribution to the Maids Under the
Mistletoe series.

ISBN: 978-0-263-07094-1

Our policy is to use papers that are natural, renewable
and recyclable products and made from wood grown in
sustainable forests. The logging and manufacturing processes
conform to the legal environmental regulations of the
country of origin.

Printed and bound in Great Britain
by CPI Antony Rowe, Chippenham, Wiltshire

For all the amazing Mills & Boon Romance
writers—past and present.

Thank you for being so welcoming to
new writers and so generous with your time,
experience and wisdom, and thank you
for writing such amazing books.

It's an honour to work with you all. x

CHAPTER ONE

Early December, Chelsea, London

'WAIT! STOP! OH, NO…' Sophie Bradshaw skidded to a halt and watched the bus sail past her, the driver utterly oblivious to her outstretched hand. 'Just great,' she muttered, pulling her cardigan more closely around her and turning, careful not to slip on the icy pavement, to scan the arrivals board in the bus stop, hoping against hope the next bus wasn't too far behind.

She huffed out a sigh of disappointment. Tonight London buses were definitely not running in pairs—she would have to wait twenty minutes until the next one. And, to add insult to injury, the light snowflakes that had been falling in a picturesque fashion over Chelsea's well-heeled streets all evening had decided to pick up both speed and strength and were now dancing dizzily through the air, blown here and there by some decidedly icy gusts of wind. Sophie eyed a taxi longingly. Would it hurt? Just this once? Only, last time she'd checked, she had only forty pounds left in her bank account, there was still a week to go until payday and, crucially, she still hadn't bought any Christmas presents.

She'd just have to wait and hope her best friend, and fellow waitress, Ashleigh, joined her soon so that she could forget her freezing hands and sore feet in a good gossip about the evening's event. Sophie hadn't received one thank you in the three hours she had toted a laden tray around the expensively dressed party-goers, but she had experienced several jostlings, three toe-tramplings and one pat on her bottom. It was a good thing her hands had been occupied in balancing the tray or the bottom patter might have found himself wearing the stuffed prawns, which would have been momentarily satisfying but probably not the best career move.

Sophie shivered as another icy gust blew through the bus shelter and straight through her inadequate if seasonally appropriate sparkly cardigan. Why hadn't she brought a coat, a proper grown-up coat with a hood and a warm lining and a waterproof outer layer? 'Vanity, thy name is Sophie,' she muttered. Well, she was getting her just reward now; nothing shrieked high-end fashion like the 'frozen drowned rat' look.

Huddling down into the cardigan, she turned, hoping once more to see her friend, but there was still no sign of Ashleigh and Sophie's phone was out of battery—again. The snow-covered street was eerily deserted, as if she were alone in the world. She blinked, hot unwanted tears filling her eyes. It wasn't just that she was cold, or that she was tired. It was that feeling of being invisible, no more human or worthy of attention than the platters she held, less interesting than the cocktails she had been handing out.

She swallowed, resolutely blinking back the tears. *Don't be a baby*, she scolded herself. So her job was hard work? At least she had a job and she was lucky enough to work with some lovely people. So her flat was so small she couldn't offer Ashleigh even a temporary home? At least she had a flat—and, even better, an almost affordable flat right here in Chelsea. Well, 'right here' being a twenty-minute bus ride away to the unfashionable edges of Chelsea, but it was all hers.

So she was a little lonely? Far, far better to be lonely alone than lonely with someone else. She knew that all too well.

She straightened her shoulders and lifted her chin as if she could physically banish her dark thoughts, but her chest still ached with a yearning for something more than the narrow existence she had lived since moving to London just over a year and a half ago. The narrow existence she'd trapped herself in long before that. What must it be like to be a guest at one of the many glittering parties and events she worked at? To wear colour and shine, not stay demure and unnoticed in black and white?

With a sigh she looked around once more, hoping that the bright smile and can-do attitude of her old friend might help her shake this sudden and unwanted melancholy, but although the snow fell thicker and faster than ever there was still no sign of Ashleigh. Nor was there any sign of the bus. The board in the shelter was resolutely sticking to an arrival in twenty minutes' time, even though at least five long minutes had already passed...

Sophie blew on her hands and thought of the warm, inviting glow of the hotel lobby just a few metres behind her. She was staff—and temporary staff at that—but surely, after a night run off her feet catering to some of the most arrogant ignoramuses she had ever had the misfortune to waitress for, they wouldn't mind her sheltering inside for just a few minutes? Besides, a snowstorm changed the rules, everyone knew that. Even a posh hotel turned into Scrooge after the three ghosts had visited, welcoming to one and all. And it would be easier to keep a lookout for Ashleigh if she wasn't constantly blinking snow out of her eyes...

Mind made up, Sophie stepped cautiously away from the limited shelter of the bus stop and onto the increasingly snowy pavement, her feet sinking with a definite crunch in the snow as she began to walk back towards the lobby. She kept her head down against the chill, picking up speed as she neared the door, and warmth was in sight when she collided with a tall figure, her heel slipping as she did so. With a surprised yelp Sophie teetered, arms windmilling as she fought to remain upright, refusing to surrender to the inevitable crash but knowing that any millisecond now she would fall…

Just as she started to lose the battle a strong hand grasped her elbow and pulled her upright. Sophie looked up, startled, and found herself staring into a pair of the darkest brown eyes she had ever seen, framed with long thick lashes. 'Careful! It's snowing. You could hurt someone—or yourself if you don't look where you're going.'

Italian, she thought dreamily. She had been saved by an Italian man with beautiful eyes. Then his sharp tone permeated the fog in her brain and she stepped back, sharply moving away from his steadying grasp.

'Snowing? So that's what this white cold stuff is. Thank you for clearing that up.' She stopped, the anger disappearing as quickly as it came as shock flared up on his face—followed by the ghost of a smile. It was a very attractive ghost;

he was probably rather gorgeous when he re-laxed. *Not relevant, Sophie.* More to the point, she *had* bumped into him. 'I'm sorry, you're right, I wasn't looking where I was going. I just wanted to get inside before I turned into the lit-tle match girl. I've had to admit defeat on find-ing transport. It's looking like I'm going to have to walk home…' She looked ruefully down at her black heels. They were surprisingly com-fortable—comfortable enough for her to wear them to work—but patent court shoes probably weren't high on most Arctic explorers' kit lists.

'Typical London, just a few flakes of snow and the taxis disappear.'

Sophie didn't want to contradict him and point out that there was a little more than a drop of snow—several inches more in fact—or that she wasn't actually looking for a taxi but for a far more prosaic bus. 'It's always the same when it snows,' she said airily, as if she were a real Lon-doner, blasé about everything, even the fairy-tale scene unfolding before her, but instantly ruined the effect by shivering.

'And you've come out inappropriately dressed.'

The disapproval was back in his voice, but before Sophie could react, he shrugged off his expensive-looking coat and wrapped it around her. 'You'll catch pneumonia if you're not careful.'

Pride warred with her frozen limbs and lost. 'I… Thank you… Although,' she couldn't help adding, 'it wasn't actually snowing when I left home.' She snuggled into the coat. The lining felt like silk and there was a distinct scent on the collar, a fresh citrus scent, sharp and very male, rather like the smartly tailored man standing in front of her. She held out her hand, just the tips of her fingers visible, peeking out of the long coat sleeves. 'Sophie Bradshaw.'

'Marco Santoro.' He took her outstretched hand and, at his touch, a fizz of attraction shivered up Sophie's spine.

She swallowed, shocked by the sudden sensation. It had been far too long since she'd had that kind of reaction and it unnerved her.

Unnerved her—but she couldn't deny a certain thrill of exhilaration too, and almost without meaning to she smiled up at him, holding his gaze boldly even as his eyes darkened with interest.

'I must be holding you up,' she said, searching for something interesting to say but settling on the banal, unsettled by the speculative look in his eyes. 'I should give you your coat back, thank you for coming to my rescue and let you get on your way.' But she couldn't quite bring herself to return the coat, not when she was so blissfully warm. Not when she was so very aware of every shifting expression on his rather-nice-to-look-at face with cheekbones cut like glaciers, the dark stubble a little too neat to be five o'clock shadow. She also rather approved of the suit, which enhanced, rather than hung off or strained over, his tall lean body. She did like a man who knew how to dress...

She'd given him the perfect getaway clause. One moment of chivalry could have marooned him here with this sharp-tongued girl for the rest of the evening. All he had to do was say thank you, retrieve his coat and be on his way. The words hovered on his tongue, but Marco paused.

There was something he rather liked about her defiantly pointed, uptilted chin, the combative spark in her blue eyes. It was a nice contrast to the tedium that had made up his evening so far.

'Take your time and warm up. I'm in no hurry. The fresh air is just what I needed after being in there.' He gestured behind him to The Chelsea Grand. 'I was at the most overcrowded, over-heated party imaginable.'

'Me too! Wasn't it awful?'

'Unbearable. What a shame I didn't see you in there. It would have brightened up a dull evening. No one ever enjoys these Export Alliance affairs, but it's necessary to show willing, don't you think?'

Her eyes flickered. 'Oh, yes, I hope the evening wasn't too much of a bore.'

Marco deliberately didn't answer straight away, running his gaze over Sophie assessingly. She was a little under average height, with silky blonde hair caught up in a neat twist. Her eyes were a clear blue, her mouth full. She wasn't as poised as his usual type, but then again he was bored of his usual type, hence the last six months' dating detox. And fate did seem to have brought them together; who was he to argue with fate? He smiled straight into her eyes. 'For a while there I thought it was. But now, maybe, it has…possibilities.'

With interest he watched her absorb his words, his meaning, colour flushing high and quick on her pale cheeks. She stepped back. 'Well, it was lovely meeting you, Mr Santoro, but I really should try to get back before I need a team of huskies to whisk me home. Thank you so much for lending me your coat. I think I'm warm enough to risk another five minutes looking for transport.'

'Or,' he suggested, 'we could wait out the storm in the comfort of a bar.' There, the gauntlet was thrown; it was up to her to take it or not.

He rather hoped she would.

Sophie opened her mouth, then closed it again. Marco could practically see the arguments running through her mind. She didn't know him. It was snowing and impossible to get home. What harm could one drink do? Was she acknowledging the sizzle of chemistry in the air? That indefinable quality that stopped him from taking his coat and walking away, that stopped her from saying a flat no. He could almost smell it, rich and ripe.

Sophie sighed, a tiny sound, a sound of capitulation. 'Thank you, a drink would be lovely.'

'*Bene*, do you know somewhere you would like to go? No? Then if I may make a suggestion, I know just the place.' He took her arm and she allowed him, as if the process of saying yes had freed her from making any more decisions. She was light under his hand, fragile as he steered her away from the hotel and down to the lights and bustle of the King's Road. Neither of them spoke, words suddenly superfluous in this winter wonderland of shadow and snow.

The bar he'd selected was just a short walk away, newly refurbished in a dazzling display of copper and light woods with long sleek tables for larger groups and hidden nooks with smaller, more intimate tables for couples. Marco steered Sophie towards the most hidden of these small areas, gesturing to the barman to bring them a bottle of Prosecco as he did so. Her eyes flickered towards his and then across their small hideaway with its low table for two, its intimate two-seater sofa, the almost hidden entrance.

'Excuse me for just a minute, I'm going to freshen up.'

'Of course, take your time.' He sat down and picked up his glass and smiled. The dull evening was suddenly alive with possibilities. Just the way he liked it.

What am I doing? What am I doing?

Sophie didn't need to look at a price list to know the bar was way out of her league—each light fitting probably cost more than every piece of furniture she owned. And she didn't need to be a mind reader to know why Marco Santoro had selected such a small, hidden table. The whole scenario had seduction written all over it.

She'd never been the kind of girl handsome men in tailored suits wanted to seduce before. What would it be like to try that girl on for size? Just for once?

The loos were as bright and trendy as the bar, with huge mirrors running all along one wall and a counter at waist height. Sophie dumped her bag onto the counter, shrugged off the coat, hanging it onto the hat stand with care, and quickly tallied up her outfit. One dress, black. One pair of tights, nude. One pair of shoes, black. One silver shrug, wet. Hair up. Make-up minimal. She could do this.

It didn't take long; it never did. Hair taken down, shaken and brushed. That was one thing about her fine, straight blonde hair: it might be boring, but it fell into place without too much effort. A colour stick added a rich berry glow to her lips and colour to her cheeks and a sweep of mascara gave her eyes some much-needed definition. A quick sweep of powder to her nose, an unflattering scarlet after ten minutes in the snow, finished her face.

She looked at herself critically. Her face was fine, her hair would do, but even though she'd added a few stitches to the Maids in Chelsea standard black dress to improve the fit, her dress was still more suitable for church than an exclusive bar. She rummaged in her bag and pulled out a white ribbon. Two seconds later she had tied it around her waist, finishing it with a chic bow. She added oversize silver hooped earrings, looped a long, twisted silver chain around her neck and held the shrug under the dryer for a minute until it was just faintly damp. Not bad. Not bad at all. She closed her bag, slung the coat nonchalantly around her shoulders and took a deep breath. It was a drink. That was all. An hour, maybe two, with someone who looked at her with interest. Someone who didn't know her, didn't feel sorry for her.

An hour, maybe two, of being someone different. A Chelsea girl, the kind of girl who went to glamorous parties and flirted with handsome men, not the kind of girl who stood on the sidelines with a tray of drinks.

Sophie wasn't remotely ashamed of what she did for a living. She worked hard and paid her own way—which was a lot more than many of the society women she cleaned for and waited on could say—and Clio, the owner of Maids in Chelsea, the agency Sophie worked for, had built up her successful business from scratch. Maids in Chelsea was known for supplying the best help in west London and Sophie and her colleagues were proud of their reputation. But it wasn't glamorous. And right now, she wanted just a few moments of glamour. To belong in the world she served and cleaned up after until the clock struck twelve and she turned back into a pumpkin.

Didn't she deserve this? It was nearly Christmas after all...

CHAPTER TWO

New Year's Eve

'THAT'S FANTASTIC, GRACE. No, of course I'm
not mad, I'm really happy for you. So when do
I get to meet him? Tonight? He's taking you to
the Snowflake Ball. That's…that's really, really
great. I can't wait. I'll see you there. Okay. Bye.
Love you.'

Sophie put her phone down and stared across
the room. If there had been room on the floor,
she would have slumped in a dramatic fashion,
but as every inch of the tiny sitting room/din-
ing room/kitchenette was covered in bolts and
scraps of fabric, she could only lean against the
wall and swallow hard.

Did Cinderella feel resentment when she was
left alone and everyone else went to the ball?
No, she was quite happy to sit by the fire with

the mice and Buttons and weave straw into gold before letting down her hair and eating an apple.

Okay. Maybe Sophie was muddling up her fairy tales a little.

But, crucially, Cinderella was excluded from the ball completely. How would she have felt if she had been made to attend the ball as a waitress and had to watch her stepsisters waltzing by in the arms of their handsome tycoons and earls? There would have been less singing, more teeth-gnashing then.

Not that Sophie had any inclination to gnash her teeth. She was happy for her friends, of *course* she was. It was amazing that they had all found such wonderful men and goodness knew they deserved their happiness—but did they all have to find true love at the same time? And did they have to find it just before the Snowflake Ball?

She sighed. Last year had been such fun, waitressing at the prestigious event with Emma and Grace, and she'd been looking forward to introducing Ashleigh to the glitter and sparkle that were the hallmarks of the charity gala. The ballroom always looked amazing, the organisers ensured there were plenty of breaks, tips were generous and there was a short staff event afterwards with champagne and a delicious buffet. In fact last year had been the best New Year's Eve Sophie could remember. But this year everything was different. First Emma had bumped into her estranged—and secret—husband, Jack Westwood, aka the Earl of Redminster, and after a few difficult weeks the pair had blissfully reconciled. Then Ashleigh had fallen for gorgeous Greek tycoon Lukas while house-sitting for him. Sophie had been over the moon when her old friend had phoned her on Christmas Eve to announce her whirlwind engagement—she'd never heard Ashleigh sound so happy.

But she had to admit that she had been a little relieved that Grace, like Sophie, was still single, still employed at Maids in Chelsea and would still be waitressing at the ball. There was only so much loved-upness a girl could take.

Only while Sophie had endured overcrowded trains back to Manchester on Christmas Eve to spend an uncomfortable two days back tiptoeing around her family's habitual disapproval and enduring the same old lectures on how she had messed up her life, Grace had spent *her* Christmas being swept off her feet by hotelier Finlay Armstrong. Swept off her feet and out of her waitress clothes and into a ballgown. She *would* be at the Snowflake Ball tonight, but, like Emma and Ashleigh, she'd be there as a guest, not hired help.

'You are officially a horrible person, Sophie Bradshaw,' Sophie said aloud. 'Grace of all people deserves all the happiness in the world.' She'd been alone in the world, even more alone than Sophie, so alone she'd chosen to work over Christmas rather than spend the holidays on her own. The rift in Sophie's family might seem irreparable, but at least she had them. Yes, Grace deserved every bit of luck and happiness the last week had brought her.

But didn't Sophie deserve some too?

She pushed herself off the wall and picked her way over to the sofa, resolving once again to do something about the material strewn all over every surface as well as the floor. She did deserve happiness; she knew that even if she didn't always feel it. Her ex, Harry, had done far too good a job of eroding every last bit of confidence from her for that. But happiness for her didn't lie in the arms of a man, no matter how titled or rich or handsome he was. It lay in her dreams. In her designs. In her… And if waitressing at this ball would help her achieve those dreams, then waitress she would—and she would smile and be happy for her friends even if they were divided from her by an invisible baize door.

Only…was Harry right? Was something wrong with her? Because she had had her own little romantic adventure this Christmas, but, unlike her friends, hers had ended when the clocks struck—well, not twelve but five a.m. It had been her choice to creep out of the hotel room without leaving as much as a note, let alone a glass slipper, but she couldn't imagine Jack or Lukas or Finlay leaving a stone unturned if their women simply disappeared without a trace. But although her heart gave the odd unwanted leap whenever she saw dark hair above an expensive suit—which in Chelsea was about thirty times a day on average—the last she had seen of Marco Santoro had been his naked, slumbering torso, dimly lit by the light of the bathroom as she had gathered her belongings together.

And okay, she hadn't looked for him either, not even when she'd confessed her one-night stand to her friends just a few days ago. Not only was Marco Santoro out of her league in every way, but Sophie had allowed infatuation to cloud her judgement before. She wasn't foolish enough to mistake lust for anything deeper, not again.

Although it had been an incredible night…

The sound of the buzzer interrupted her slide into reminiscences just as she was picturing the curve of Marco's mouth. Sophie shivered as she pushed the all too real picture away and picked up the answerphone. 'Yes?'

'Sophie, it's me, Ashleigh.' Her old friend's unmistakably Australian tones sang out of the intercom and Sophie's spirits immediately lifted. So all her friends would be married to insanely wealthy, influential and hot men? It wouldn't really make a difference, not where it counted most.

'Come on up.' She pressed the buzzer and looked around wildly. Was it possible to clear a space in just twenty seconds? There was a knock on the door before she had managed to do more than pick up several scraps of material and, with them still clasped in her hand, Sophie opened the door to discover not just Ashleigh but Grace and Emma as well, brandishing champagne and a thick white envelope.

'Surprise!' they sang out in chorus, surging into the room in a wave of perfume, silk and teetering heels. The dress code for the Snow-flake Ball was white or silver, but blonde, tall Emma had added red shoes and accessories to her long white silk shift, Grace, glowing with happiness, was sultry in silver lace and Ashleigh had opted for a backless ivory dress, which set off the copper in her hair and the green in her eyes. They all looked gorgeous. Sophie tried not to look over at her black waitress's dress, ironed and hung on the back of the door.

'How lovely to see you all.' She narrowed her eyes at Grace. 'You must have called me from just around the corner.'

'From the taxi,' Grace confirmed, her eyes laughing.

'Congratulations again. Finlay's a lucky man and I'll tell him so when I finally meet him. I'd hug you, but I don't want to crease your dress.'

'Where are the glasses?' Emma, of course, was already at the counter optimistically known as a kitchenette looking in one of the three narrow cupboards allotted for crockery and food. 'Aha!' She brandished them triumphantly, setting them down before twisting the foil off the bottle. It was real champagne, Sophie noted, a brand well out of her price bracket. Funny to think just a few weeks ago they would have happily been drinking cheap cava from the off-licence at the end of her street. So the divide between her lifestyle and her friends' had begun. Just as it had ten years ago when she had opted for paid work and domesticity while her few friends went to university.

She pushed the thought away as the champagne cork was expertly popped. 'Not for me, Em. I can't. You know what Clio says about drinking on the job and I need to be at the hotel for staff briefing in an hour.'

'Now, that,' Ashleigh said triumphantly, 'is where you are wrong. We've asked Keisha to cover your shift and you, Miss Sophie Bradshaw, will be going to the ball! Here you are, a formal invitation.' She thrust the envelope towards Sophie, who took it mechanically.

'I've always wanted to be a fairy godmother,' Grace said, holding out her hand to accept one of the full glasses Emma was handing out.

Sophie stared at the three beaming faces, completely flabbergasted as she took in their words, the envelope still clutched unopened in her hand. 'I'm what?'

'Going to the Snowflake Ball!'

'We're taking you as our guest!'

'You didn't think we'd leave you out, did you?' Ashleigh finished, taking a glass from Emma and pressing it into Sophie's unresisting hand. 'Cheers!'

'But…but…my hair. And what will I wear?'

'Oh, I don't know,' Emma said. 'If only one of us was an aspiring fashion designer with a wardrobe crammed full of original designs. Hang on a minute…' She strode into the minuscule bedroom—so tiny Sophie could only fit in a single cabin bed—and pulled back the curtain that divided the crammed clothes rails from the rest of the room. 'Ta-dah!'

'I couldn't wear one of my designs to an event like this! Everyone else will be in dresses like, well, like yours. Expensive, designer…'

'And you will outshine us all in an original Sophie Bradshaw.' Grace beamed at her. 'Oh, Sophie, it's going to be a magical night. I am so very happy you are coming with is. Let's get you ready…'

Why on earth did I agree to attend this ball?

More to the point, why did he agree to attend the Snowflake Ball every New Year's Eve? It was always the same, filled with the same people, the same talk, the same tedium. Marco cast a scowling look at the crowded ballroom. Oh, it was tastefully done out with abstract snowflakes suspended from the ceiling and the glitter kept to a minimum, but it was still not a patch on Venice on New Year's Eve. His was a city that knew how to celebrate and New Year was a night when the stately old city came alive.

He hadn't spent a New Year in Venice for over a decade, although there were times when the pull of the city of his birth ran through his veins like the water in the canals and he missed the alleyways and bridges, the grand old *palazzos* and the markets with an almost physical ache that no amount of excellent champagne and food could make up for. His hands folded into fists. Tomorrow he would return home, not just for a fleeting visit, some business and a duty dinner with his mother and sister. Tomorrow he would return for a fortnight, to host the Santoros' annual Epiphany Ball and then stay to walk his sister down the aisle.

Tomorrow he would step into his father's shoes, no matter that he wasn't ready. No matter that he didn't deserve to.

Marco took a deep sip of wine, barely tasting the richness. He wouldn't think about it tonight, his last night of freedom. He needed a distraction.

His eyes skimmed the room, widening with

appreciation as four women stopped at a table opposite. They were talking over each other, faces lit with enthusiasm as they took their seats. His gaze lingered on a laughing blonde. Her silver minidress was an interesting choice in what was a mainly conservatively dressed ballroom, but Marco wasn't complaining, not when the wearer possessed such excellent legs. Excellent legs, a really nice, lithe figure and, as she turned to face him as if she were aware of his scrutiny, a pair of familiar blue eyes. Eyes staring straight back at him with such undisguised horror Marco almost turned and checked, just to make sure there wasn't an axe murderer creeping up behind him.

The girl from the snow. The one who had disappeared...

Marco muttered a curse, unsure whether to coolly acknowledge her or ignore her presence; it had been a novel experience to wake up and find himself alone without as much as a note. Novel and not exactly pleasant; in Marco's experience women clung on long after the relationship was over, they didn't disappear before it had even begun.

And they certainly didn't run away before dawn.

His eyes narrowed. She owed him an explanation at the least, apology at best. There were rules for these kinds of encounters and Sophie Bradshaw had broken every one. Besides, he was damned if he was going to spend the evening marked as the big bad wolf with Little Silver Dress going all wide-eyed at the very sight of him. He had a fortnight of difficult encounters ahead of him; tonight was supposed to be about having fun.

Mind made up, Marco took a step in Sophie's direction, but she was already on her feet and shouldering her way through the ballroom. Away from him. So she liked to play, did she? He set off at an unhurried pace, following the silver dress as it darted across the crowded room and through a discreet door set in the wooden panelling. The door began to close behind her, but his long stride shortened the distance enough for him to catch it before it could close fully and he slipped inside…

To find himself inside a closet. A large closet, but a closet nonetheless, one filled with towering stacks of spare chairs, folded tables and several cleaning trolleys. Sophie was pressed against one of the tables, her hands gripping the sides, her heart-shaped face pale.

He allowed the door to close behind him, leaning against it, his arms folded, staring her down. '*Buongiorno*, Sophie.'

'Marco? Wh-what are you doing here?'

'Catching up with old friends. That's what I like about these occasions, you never know who you might bump into. Nice corner you've found here. A little crowded, lacking in decoration, but I like it.'

'I…' Her eyes were wide. Scared.

Incredulity thundered through him. He'd assumed she had hidden because she was embarrassed to see him, that maybe she hadn't told her friends—or boyfriend—about him. Or because she was playing some game and trying to lure him in. It hadn't occurred to him that she would be actually terrified at the very thought of seeing him.

Although she had fled from his bed, run away from her friends the moment she had recognised him. How many clues did he need? His mouth compressed into a thin line. 'Apologies, Sophie,' he said stiffly. 'I didn't mean to scare you. Please rest assured that I will leave you alone for the rest of the evening.' He bowed formally and turned, hand on the door handle, only to be arrested by the sound of her low voice.

'No, Marco. I should apologise. I didn't expect to see you here, I didn't expect to see you ever again actually and I overreacted. I'm not… I don't really do… You know. What we did. I have no idea how these things work.'

What we did. Marco had spent the last three weeks trying to put what they'd done out of his mind. Tried not to dwell on the satin of her skin, the taste of her, the way she laughed. The way she moaned.

Ironically he usually did know how these things worked. Temporary and discreet were the hallmarks of the perfect relationship as far as

Marco was concerned. Not falling into bed with strangers he'd met on street corners. He was far too cautious. He needed to be certain that any and every prospective partner knew the rules: mutually satisfying and absolutely no strings.

But somehow that evening all his self-imposed rules had gone flying out of the window. It had been like stepping into another world; the snow deep outside, the city oddly muted, the world contracting until it was only the two of them. It seemed as if there had been no other route open to him, booking the hotel room an unsaid inevitability as they'd moved on to their second drink, walking hand in hand through the falling snow but not really touching, not yet, waiting until the room door had swung closed behind them.

And then...

Marco inhaled, the heat of that night burning through his body. He didn't know what he'd have done if she'd been there when he woke up, pulled her to him or distanced himself in the cold light of day. But he hadn't had to make that decision; like the melted snow outside, she was gone. He'd told himself it was for the best. But now that she was here, it was hard to remember why.

He turned. Sophie was still staring at him, her blue eyes huge in her pale face. 'How these things work?' he repeated, unable to stop the smile curving his mouth. 'Does there have to be a set path?'

Colour flared high on her cheekbones. 'No, I'm not looking for Mr Right, but neither am I the kind of girl who spends the night with a stranger. Usually. So I don't know what the etiquette is here.'

'Nor do I, but I'm pretty sure it doesn't require us to spend half the evening in a cleaning closet.'

'No,' she said doubtfully as if the cleaning closet were actually the perfect place to spend New Year's Eve. 'But what happens when we get out there? Do we acknowledge that we know each other or pretend that none of it ever happened?'

The latter was certainly the most sensible idea—but hadn't he decided he needed a distraction? Sophie Bradshaw in a silver minidress was the epitome of distraction. Marco stepped away from the door, leaving it a little ajar, and smiled as ruefully as he could. 'Are those my choices? They seem a little limited. How about I throw a third option in there—I ask you to dance?'

'Ask me to dance?' Her eyes were even wider than before if that was possible and she pressed even further into the table. 'But I walked out on you. Without a note! And I ran away as soon as I saw you.'

'*Sì*, both of these things are true, but if you dance with me, then I am willing to overlook both transgressions.'

'I did mention that I don't want a relationship, didn't I?'

'You did. Sophie, I am also not looking for anything serious and, like you, I'm not in the habit of picking up strangers in the snow. So if neither of us is interested in a relationship and neither of us indulges in one-night stands, then why not get to know each other better? Retrospectively. Unless you're here with someone else?' His hands curled into loose fists at the thought, the thrill of possession taking him by surprise. It was only because they had barely scratched the surface of their attraction, he reminded himself. Only because spending the evening with Sophie would be safe and yet satisfying. No expectations beyond fun and flirtation, although if the evening did end the same way as their past encounter, he wouldn't complain. His gaze travelled down the sixties-inspired minidress to the acres of shapely leg, lingering on the slight swell of her hips. No, he wouldn't be complaining at all.

'No. I'm here with my friends and their husbands and fiancés. They are all lovely and doing their best to include me, but they're all so madly, sickeningly in love that I can't help feeling like a spare part.'

She was wavering. Time to press his advantage. 'Then this is fate,' he said promptly. 'Every time you feel like a spare part, dance with me. We can have a code.'

Her eyebrows raised. 'A code?'

'*Sì*, you rub your nose or tug your ear and I will know you need rescuing from the tedium of romance.'

'They don't mean to be tedious.' But the wariness had disappeared from her face and she was smiling. 'What if you're not watching, when I signal?'

'Oh, I'll be watching,' he assured her. 'But just in case you forget to signal, let's make an appointment now to see the new year in together. I'll meet you...' He paused, trying to think of a landmark in the ballroom.

'Outside this closet?'

'Perfect. Yes, I'll meet you outside here at eleven.'

'But that's a whole hour before midnight.'

'You owe me half an hour of dancing for running out on me and half an hour for escaping into a closet. I'm Italian, the hurt to my *machismo* could have been catastrophic.'

A dimple flashed in her cheek. 'Okay, eleven it is. Unless I need rescuing, in which case I'll... I'll twizzle my hair. Deal?'

'Deal.' Marco opened the door and held it, standing to one side while Sophie passed through it, brushing past him as she did so, his body exploding into awareness at each point she touched. He took her hand as he stepped out of the small room and raised it to his lips. 'Until eleven, *signorina*. I look forward to further making your acquaintance.'

Marco leaned against the door as he watched Sophie disappear back into the ballroom. Yes, she would do very nicely as a distraction, very nicely indeed. Suddenly he was looking forward to the rest of the Snowflake Ball after all.

CHAPTER THREE

'WHO IS THAT HOTTIE? What?' Emma looked round at her friends, indignation flashing in her eyes at their splutters. 'I'm married, blissfully and happily married, but I still have eyes—and, Sophie…that man is sizzling. Tell us all.'

Sophie slid into her seat uncomfortably aware that her cheeks were probably bright red under her friends' scrutiny. 'There's nothing to tell,' she said, picking up her white linen napkin, dislodging a drift of small glittery paper snow-flakes as she did so. 'I didn't miss the starter, did I? I'm starving.'

'Tell me my eyes are deceiving me and I didn't just see you emerge from a closet with him.' Ashleigh leaned in to stare intently at her and Sophie's cheeks got even hotter if that was possible—she was almost combusting as it was. 'Ha!

You did. Nice work, Soph. Quick work though. We've only been here for twenty minutes.'

'I didn't go *into* the closet with him.' Sophie reached for her glass of champagne and took a much-needed sip, wincing at the unexpectedly dry taste. She pushed it aside and grabbed some water instead. 'He followed me in there.'

'He did what? I take it back. He's not hot. He's creepy. Well, kind of both. Do you want me to set Jack on him?'

'I'm sure Lukas would be only too glad to have a word,' Ashleigh chimed in with a dark look over at the corner Marco had disappeared into.

'Finlay can be very intimidating,' Grace said, smiling dreamily at her very new and very large pink diamond ring on the third finger of her left hand.

'No, thanks for the offer, but I don't need defending.' Sophie lowered her voice. 'I know him. He's the guy…'

Three faces stared at her blankly.

She sighed. It wasn't as if there had been many—or indeed any—guys since she'd moved to London. 'The guy. From a few weeks ago. The export party guy. You know, in the snow… Italian, we went to a bar…'

'Oh, the one-night-stand guy?' Ashleigh exclaimed.

'Just a little louder, Ash, I don't think he heard you over on the other side of the room, but just one more decibel should do it.'

'What's he doing here? It must be fate.'

'No, Grace, it's not fate. It's embarrassing, that's what it is. I didn't expect to see him again, that's the whole *point* of a one-night stand.'

'Ah, but the real question is are you going to see him again? Now that he's the one-night stand and the quickie-in-the-closet guy?' Emma's eyes were twinkling.

'We did not have a quickie in the closet. Your mind! Call yourself a Countess?'

'It's My Lady to you.' But Emma's smile was rueful. Her friends hadn't got tired of teasing her about her newly acquired title. Sophie wasn't sure they ever would.

'You didn't answer the question, Sophie. Are you going to see him again?'

'Look, just because the three of you are all besotted doesn't mean that I'm looking to settle down. I've been there and done that and it very much didn't agree with me. I have agreed to dance with him later. But that's all I want. Honestly.'

But the scepticism on all three faces showed that none of them believed her. And she didn't blame them because she wasn't entirely sure she believed herself. Oh, she didn't want or need what her friends had, she wasn't hankering after a diamond ring the size of Ashleigh's or Emma's, nor, beautiful as it was, did she want to wear Grace's huge pink diamond. She was quite happy with a ring-free third finger, thank you very much. In fact Sophie's ambitions were as far from domestic bliss as it was possible to get. She wanted to make something of herself. Prove to her family—prove to herself—that she hadn't thrown her life, her chances away when she'd moved in with Harry. She didn't have the time or the inclination for romance.

But shocking as it had been to see Marco, it hadn't been unpleasant. After all, Emma was right: he was smoking hot. Smoking hot and charming. Smoking hot, charming and very, very good in bed. Not that she was planning to sleep with him again. Once was an excusable lapse, twice would be something far too much like a relationship.

But a dance wouldn't hurt—would it?

Sophie had had no intention of using any of the secret signs Marco had suggested. She kept her hands firmly on her lap, on her knife and fork, or wrapped around her water glass to ensure that she didn't inadvertently summon him over. But, as the night wore on, her resolve wavered. It wasn't that her friends and their partners intentionally excluded her, but they just couldn't help themselves. They kept separating off into cosy little pairs to sway intimately on the dance floor, no matter what the music, or to indulge in some very public displays of affection over the smoked salmon starter. In some ways it was worse when they emerged from their love-struck idyll and remembered Sophie's presence, tumbling over themselves to apologise and making Sophie feel even more like a third—or seventh—wheel than ever.

Then when the men sauntered off to the bar between courses, leaving the four friends alone, the conversation turned, inevitably Sophie supposed, to Grace's and Ashleigh's forthcoming weddings.

'Definitely a church wedding,' Grace said. 'Probably in Scotland, although it would be a shame not to hold the reception at The Armstrong. After all, that's where we met. The only thing is a church can be a little limiting. Do you think it would be okay for the bridesmaids to wear short dresses in a church?'

'The bridesmaids were in minidresses at the last church wedding I attended. They were certainly effective.' So effective that Harry, Sophie's ex, hadn't been able to take his eyes off the head bridesmaid as she had paraded down the aisle all tumbled hair and bronzed, lithe legs. Nor, it had transpired just a few hours later, had he been able to keep his hands off her either. Sophie swallowed, reaching for her water blindly to try to mask the metallic taste she always noticed when she thought about that night. The taste of humiliation. Not just because Harry had treated her like that; if she was honest with herself, he'd behaved like that for far too many years. Nor was it because he had chosen to do so in front of all of their friends; after all, Sophie had spent many occasions making excuses for him or turning a well-practised blind eye. No, the scalding shame she still experienced every day was because it had taken such a blatant humiliation to force her to act, to realise that this bad boy couldn't be redeemed and he wasn't worth one more of her tears.

How had it taken seven years? Her parents had known it almost instantly, as had her few friends. And yet she'd chosen Harry over every single one of them, sure that she saw something special in him nobody else could see. Maybe if she'd been more confident, maybe if she hadn't felt so alone when she met him…

No, there were no maybes. She had only herself to blame. What a fool, young and blinded by lust and romance. Never again.

She looked over at her friends, forcing a smile.

'I have a request, no, a demand. You must promise to seat me at a table full of fabulous, fun single ladies. No set-ups with your cousin's best friend's brother's boss just because he visited Manchester once and so we'll have lots in common and no nudging me towards the best man because that's what happens at weddings. I want a party table.'

'It's a promise,' Ashleigh agreed, turning to greet Lukas with a brilliant smile as he put another champagne-filled ice bucket down on the table along with another bottle of mineral water. Maybe she was too used to cheap cava, but Sophie just couldn't drink the champagne; every sip tasted sour. Not only was she a third wheel, but she was a sober third wheel...

What was wrong with her? She *should* be having a good time; she looked okay, her dress had got several appreciative comments, which was always warming to a designer's ears, the food was really tasty, the band talented and the ballroom looked like a very tasteful winter wonderland. It was New Year's Eve and she was out with her best friends being wined and dined.

Sophie straightened. She was being selfish. She shouldn't need anything more.

Except…

Sophie's gaze slid, not for the first time, over to the large round table at the other side of the room. Marco was leaning back in his chair, a glass clasped elegantly in his fingertips, apparently deeply involved in a conversation with the couple sat next to him. Only a slight inclination of the head and a tilt of the glass towards her in a light toast betrayed his awareness of her scrutiny. But he knew, she had no doubt. He'd known every time.

It was only nine o'clock. Two hours until their promised dance.

The third of the six courses had been cleared away and Emma and Jack had taken advantage of the hiatus in the meal to dance—if you called moving very slowly staring intensely at each other dancing. Grace and Finlay were sitting opposite Sophie, but there was no point trying to chat to either of them; they were looking into each other's eyes, emitting so much heat Sophie had moved the water jug closer in case they suddenly combusted. As for Ashleigh, Sophie hadn't seen her friend for several minutes, but at last sight she had been towing Lukas determinedly towards the closet Sophie had discovered earlier.

She had a choice. She could spend the next two hours sitting here feeling sorry for herself or she could allow herself some real fun. The kind of fun she'd been too busy accommodating Harry to enjoy before. The kind of fun she hadn't allowed herself since the breakup. Just looking at Marco made her stomach fall away and her breath hitch, but she was no longer a naïve teenager who couldn't tell the difference between lust and love. And that was what this was: pure and simple delicious lust. If she knew that, remembered that, then what harm could a few more hours in Marco's company do?

And as the thought crossed her mind her hand rose, almost by its own volition, and, with her eyes fixed on Marco, Sophie slowly and deliberately wound a lock of hair around her finger and smiled.

* * *

He'd been aware of her every second of the evening, from the moment she'd walked away from him to rejoin her friends. The swish of her hair, the sway of her hips, the curve of her mouth. It was as if an invisible thread stretched across the vast room connecting them; every time she moved he felt it, a deep visceral pull.

It was unlike any reaction he'd ever had towards a woman and it wasn't hard to work out why; he didn't need a degree in psychology to realise that she was probably the first woman to walk away from him and he was completely unaccustomed to not calling the shots in all his relationships, personal and professional. No wonder his interest was piqued.

Not that he wanted her to know it. Knowledge was power in every relationship, no matter how temporary.

But Marco knew every time Sophie slid a look in his direction, he felt the tension in her as if it were his, he knew she would cave in eventually and so, with a surge of triumph, he watched her as she reached up and wound a lock of silky blonde hair around her finger, a provocative smile on her full mouth—and a challenge in her eyes.

Marco's expectations of the evening had risen the second he'd caught sight of the elusive Signorina Bradshaw; at that look in her eyes they took flight. 'Excuse me,' he said, pushing his chair back and languidly getting to his feet. No need to rush. She wasn't going anywhere. 'I have some personal business to attend to.'

He held Sophie's gaze as he moved with predatory grace across the dance floor, his steps slow and easy until he came to a halt in front of her. Sophie sat alone on one side of the table, the only other occupants breaking off from an intense conversation to watch, open-mouthed, as he extended a hand. *'Signorina?'*

Sophie arched an elegant bow. 'Sir?'

He smiled at that, slow and purposeful. 'Would you do me the honour?'

'How very unexpected.' Her eyes laughed up at him. 'I don't know what to say.'

'I believe the words you are looking for are "Thank you. I would love to."'

'Are they? In that case thank you, I would love to.' And she slipped her hand into his and allowed him to lead her from her chair and onto the dance floor.

She slipped into his arms as if she had never left, every curve fitting perfectly against him, her arms resting naturally around his waist. 'Are you having a nice evening?' It was a strangely formal question considering the way her body was pressed to his.

'I am now,' Marco answered gravely and, with some satisfaction, watched the colour rise in her cheeks. 'Have you attended this ball before?'

'I was here last year.'

'No, I was here also. How on earth did I miss you? Impossible.'

She smiled, a dimple peeping out. He remembered that dimple; it had enchanted him the first time she had smiled, snowflakes tangled in her hair, slipping on the snowy ground. 'Maybe you weren't looking hard enough. So this is a regular event for you?'

He shrugged. 'Usually. One of my clients always has a table and so here I am.'

'How very convenient. Don't you want to...' But she trailed off, shaking her head. 'Never mind.'

'Don't I want to what?'

'I'm just being nosy. It's just, isn't spending New Year with clients a little, well, impersonal? What about your friends and family?'

His stomach clenched. Tomorrow would be all about family—with one glaring omission. 'My clients are my friends as well, of course. Most of the people I know in the UK I met through work. What about you? Who are the people you are here with?'

The dimple peeked out again. 'Work friends,' she admitted. 'London can be a lonely place when you first move here.'

'You're not from London?'

'Manchester, and no, I'm not spending New Year with my family either. I did Christmas and that was more than enough.' A shadow crossed her face so fleetingly he wondered if he'd imagined it. 'How about you? Whereabouts in Italy are you from?'

'Venice.'

Her eyes lit up. 'Oh, how utterly gorgeous. What an amazing place to live.'

Amazing, thrilling, beautiful, hidebound, full of rules and expectations no man could be expected to keep. 'You've been?'

'Well, no. But I've read about it, watched films, seen pictures. It's at the top of my bucket list—lying back in a gondola and watching the canals go by. Masked balls, *palazzos*, bridges...' She laughed. 'Listen to me, I sound like such a tourist.'

'No, no. It is a beautiful city. You should go.'

'One day.' She sounded wistful. 'How can you bear to live here when you could live there? London is cool and all, but Venice? There's a story, a view around every corner.'

'And a member of my family, or an old family friend, or their relative. *Sì*...' as her eyes widened in understanding '...Venice is beautiful, captivating, unique, all these things and I miss it every day, but it is also an island. A very small island.'

'Gets a little claustrophobic?'

'A little. But London? Here a man can be who

he wants to be, see who he wants to see, do the work he feels fitting. Be his own man.'

'London's not that big,' she pointed out. 'After all, I've bumped into you twice—literally the first time!'

'Ah, but, *signorina*...' he leaned forward so his breath touched her ear and felt her shiver at the slight contact '...that was fate and we don't question the workings of fate.'

They were so close he could feel her heart racing against him before she pulled back. 'Still, small or not, it must be a wonderful place to live. Are your parents still there?'

'My mother,' he corrected her. 'My father died ten months ago.' He steeled himself for the usual hit of guilt, regret and anger. Guilt his father's heart had been weakened in the first place, regret they had never patched up their relationship—and anger his father would never now admit that Marco had a right to a life of his own.

'Ten months ago? That's so recent, I'm sorry.'

'Thank you.'

'She must miss you, your mother.'

He allowed a smile but knew it was wintry at

best. 'Miss me? I'm not sure. Miss telling me how to live my life? Every day.'

'I know a little about that. What does your mother want that's so terrible?'

Marco shrugged. 'What every Italian mother wants for her children, especially her only son. A place in the family business under her eyes, a wife, children, the usual.'

'And you aren't hankering for *bambinos* clustered around your knee?' She didn't sound disappointed or disapproving, which made a refreshing change. So many women seemed to see Marco's lack of interest in a family as a personal affront—or, worse, a challenge. 'Sunday morning football, wet wipes in every pocket? I have two brothers and they both have kids. I know the drill.'

'I like my life the way it is. Why complicate it?'

'And I take it no interest in a wife either.' She smiled, a small dimple charming him as she did so. 'Your poor mother.'

'She only has herself to blame,' he said lightly. 'My marriage is an obsession with her. I remember going to my mother's friend's house and while the mothers talked I played with the daughter. She was a nice girl, sporty. We got on really well. When we left my *mamma* asked me if I liked her and when I said I did she said *bene* she would make a good wife for me. I was five!'

'All mothers do that. My mother was convinced I'd marry Tom next door. He played the violin and sang in the church choir, always said hello and helped shovel snow or rake leaves. Perfect husband material.'

'And yet he isn't here with you tonight?'

'Well, it turns out that Tom prefers boys to girls, so even if I had been tempted, it was never going to happen.'

'Lucky for me.' He pulled Sophie in close and swung her around. 'Tell me, *signorina*, why are we here in this beautiful room dancing to this beautiful music and discussing my mother? I can think of many more interesting topics.'

Her eyes laughed up at him. 'Such as?'

'Such as how very sexy you look in that dress. Such as how very well you dance. Such as what shall we do with all this time until midnight?'

Sophie swallowed, her eyes luminous in the bright, pulsing disco lights. His eyes were drawn to the graceful column of her neck, the lines of her throat, and he ran his thumb down her skin, feeling her pulse speed up. 'Do?' she echoed a little hoarsely. 'Why, *signor*, you asked me to dance and so far we've just swayed to the music. Less talk, more dancing. It's New Year's Eve after all.'

There was no conversation after that, just dancing, movement, an intimacy that could only be conjured by two bodies caught up in the same beat. Sophie could *move*, hair flying, eyes shining and silver minidress glittering in the disco lights as she swayed and turned. 'A childhood full of dance lessons,' she told him during a breathless break. 'I did it all, ballet, jazz, tap. I have medals and everything.'

But as the night neared midnight the music slowed and she was back in his arms. The ballroom was filled with anticipation as the seconds began to tick away, people gathering in groups ready to welcome in the new year. Marco steered Sophie to a secluded corner of the dance floor, not wanting the shared jollity, the drunken group embraces that so often marked the new year's first seconds. *'Felice anno nuovo.'*

'Happy New Year, Marco.' Her eyes were half shuttered, her lips full and inviting. He knew the taste of them, the sweet plumpness of her bottom lip, knew the way her hands wound into his hair as a kiss deepened, how her skin slid like silk under his fingertips. Just a dance, he'd said. Surely they'd both known that after the night they had shared they couldn't possibly stop at dancing. Besides, it was New Year's Eve; it was customary to kiss.

And how he hated to be rude. Just one kiss, to round off the evening, to round off their brief but, oh, so pleasing acquaintanceship.

Sophie purred her approval as he lowered his mouth to hers, her hands tightening on his shoulders, her body swaying closer until he felt every curve pressed tight against him. Marco was dimly aware that the room was erupting with cheers as the new year dawned, could hear bangs and pops as the balloons and streamers were released and the first chords of 'Auld Lang Syne' began to echo around the room, but it was as if he and Sophie were separated from the cheerful celebration, hidden in some alternate dimension where all he knew was her mouth under his, her body quivering under his caress, her touch on his neck, light enough to drive a man mad.

And then it was over as she stepped back, trembling and wide-eyed. 'Thank you for a lovely night. I don't think...I mean, my friends will be looking for me.'

It took a few moments for her words to penetrate his fogged-up brain. All he wanted was to pull her back in, take her mouth again, hold her still. Marco inhaled, long and deep, pushing the dangerous desire deep down where it belonged.

'It was my pleasure. I am glad I got to meet you again, *signorina*.' He took her hand, bowing formally over it, then stepped back, a final farewell. She hesitated for the briefest of seconds and then, with a quick smile, turned away.

A pleasant interlude and now it was over as all these interludes eventually were. Unless...

Tomorrow he returned home. Returned to a wedding, to play a part, to the weight of parental expectations, no less heavy with the loss of his father. Returned to guilt.

He could do with a distraction.

Sophie obviously wasn't looking for any kind of relationship; in fact this was the third time she'd walked away from him without a backwards glance. A wry smile curved his mouth; thank goodness her response to his kiss had been so all encompassing or he'd be wondering if the attraction was one-sided. And she had never seen Venice…

She would make the perfect distraction, for himself and for his family.

Marco didn't want to take any more time to think his idea through, not when Sophie was disappearing into the revelling crowd. 'Sophie?' She stopped and turned, a confused expression on her face.

He crossed the distance between them with a few long strides. 'My mother will be holding her annual party on the sixth of January, for Epiphany. I have to be there, to co-host, in place of my father. Would you like to be my guest?'

The confusion deepened. 'Me? Come to Venice? But…'

'You said yourself how much you want to go.'

'Yes.' She looked tempted for a moment, then frowned again. 'But, Marco, I hardly know you. You don't know me and I'm not really looking for anything, for anyone. I like you, I like spending time with you…'

'And I like spending time with you and I really would like to get to know you better. And that's all this is, Sophie. A couple of days in Venice, a party and then we go our separate ways. What do you say?'

'Of course you should say yes.' The ball might officially be over for another year, but the evening was far from finished yet—after all, as Emma pointed out, they hadn't properly celebrated Grace's engagement yet—and so they had all piled into taxis and gone back to The Armstrong, the hotel Finlay owned and where the newly engaged couple had met, to finish welcoming the new year in in style. It was a novel experience for Sophie to be escorted up to the exclusive suite as a guest, not a maid, and to sink onto one of the comfortable sofas, the room-service menu at her disposal and the promise of a car to take her home.

A novel experience for Sophie, but all her friends seemed to take this level of luxury almost for granted; even Grace stepped into the private lift as if it were an everyday occurrence for her. And now it was. Grace, just like Ashleigh and Emma, was marrying into some serious wealth.

This evening, lovely as it was, was exposing the very clear differences in Sophie's future and the paths her friends were headed down—and made her even more determined to shape hers the way she had always intended it to be. This year she'd put some serious effort into the website she'd recently set up and start trying to sell her designs. She clenched her hands at the familiar twist of excitement and fear. What if Harry was right? What if she was wasting her time?

Grace plumped down onto the sofa opposite, heaving her bare feet onto the glass coffee table with a sigh of relief. 'I agree. Go, have fun. It's always quiet at work at this time of year—and we've been run off our feet for months. Take some time off. You deserve it.'

'I'll lend you the fare if you need it. Consider it an early birthday present.' Ashleigh seated herself next to Sophie and nudged her. 'Venice, Soph. You've always wanted to go.'

'Marco offered to pay for my ticket. No, don't look so excited. He has loads of air miles from his work. It's not a big deal.' Actually it was. Sophie didn't want to admit how much his casual 'I'll cover all expenses, it's the least I can do, you'll be far more of a help than you realise' had touched her. Harry had not only always expected Sophie to pay her way but frequently his as well. He was a musician after all, above mundane worldly tasks like making a living. 'It's just, I hardly know him.'

Grace raised her eyebrows knowingly. 'Didn't look that way from where I was sitting tonight. The chemistry between you two...*oof*!' She fanned herself dramatically, ducking with a squeal as Sophie threw a cushion at her.

'What do you need to know?' Ashleigh asked,

squeezing Sophie's hand. 'What would make you feel better about going?'

Sophie shrugged, unable to articulate the prickle of unease that ran over her when she thought about accepting Marco's casual invitation—or, more worryingly, the ripple of excitement overshadowing the unease. 'I don't know where he lives. I don't exactly know what he does for a living. I don't know if he likes music or books or walks in the country.'

'What *do* you know?' Emma curled up next to Grace. 'Tell us about him.'

'He's Italian, does something to do with art and antiques. Erm…he's lived in London for ages but really loves Venice, you can hear it in his voice. He has a gorgeous accent, dresses really well, his suits look handmade to me, beautifully designed, great fabric.'

'Focus, Sophie. We want to know about the man, not his clothes. How does he make you feel?'

How did he make her *what*? When Sophie had packed her bags, the shattered remaining pieces of her pride and her bruised heart and moved over a hundred miles away to start again, the one thing she had guarded herself against was feeling too much. It was thanks to her emotions she had fallen into such a sorry state in the first place. She picked up a cushion and cradled it close, as if it were a shield between her and the rest of the world while she thought. 'He makes me feel sexy. Wanted. Powerful.' Where had those words come from? But even as she spoke them Sophie knew that they were the truth— and that not once, in seven years, had Harry made her feel any of those things. Desperate, insecure, weak, needy, pathetic? All the above. Never powerful. Never wanted.

She straightened, turning to stare at Ashleigh half excited, half terrified. 'I should go, shouldn't I?'

'You should totally go. Who cares about his address and what exactly something in art and antiques means? As long as he isn't a drug smuggler and doesn't live with his wife and six kids, it's irrelevant. Sexy and powerful? Now, *they're* relevant.'

'Who knows where it might lead? Look at me.

I went to Scotland for a bit of adventure and came back head over heels. Go for it!' Grace practically clapped in excitement, but Sophie shook her head emphatically.

'I am so happy for you, Grace, for all of you. But believe me, I'm not going to come back engaged. Marco made it very clear he's not interested in anything long-term and that suits me perfectly. There's a lot I want to achieve, that I need to achieve, and wedded bliss is very far down that list. But this will be good for me. I've been so scared of being sucked back into a relationship I've gone too far the other way. This is a big city. I should date and see people occasionally, live a little.'

'Live a lot,' Emma corrected her. 'You should, Sophie, you deserve to. And we'll be cheering you on every step of the way.'

CHAPTER FOUR

'LIVE A LOT,' Sophie reminded herself as she passed through the customs gate and into the arrivals hall. Her new mantra. She'd been repeating it throughout the flight, torn between excitement at seeing Venice—and Marco—at last and apprehension about the next few days. What if she and Marco had nothing to say to each other now she was here, or what if his mother didn't like her?

No, those negative thoughts were old Sophie, not new, improved, positive, life-grabbing Sophie. Pushing them aside, she scanned the arrivals hall, impatient to see Marco. She hadn't spoken to him since New Year's Eve as he had flown out the very next day, but he had sent an itinerary with her ticket and promised that she would be met at the airport.

Maybe he was running late…

As she scanned the waiting crowd again a sign bearing a familiar name caught her eye and, as she paused to read it again, the bearer, a slight man in his forties, formally dressed in a chauffeur's uniform and cap, caught her eye and smiled. 'Signorina Bradshaw?' he asked in heavily accented but perfect English. 'Signor Santoro asked me to meet you. He has been called away.' He handed Sophie an envelope as he deftly relieved her of her suitcase and bag.

Disappointment warred with a cowardly relief. Work had predictably been quiet over the last few days, leaving Sophie far too much time to second-guess her decision and, even though she'd tried to bury herself in her designs or wrestle with the unnecessarily complicated content management system on her still-not-live website, she often found herself sitting still staring into space, her heart thumping with panic at the prospect of stepping outside the narrow life she'd built herself.

The envelope was thick, more like an invitation than a piece of office stationery, and it took Sophie a couple of moments to open it and pull

out a piece of crisp white paper. She unfolded it
and scanned the brief lines.

Sophie,
Please accept my most sincere apologies but
I am unavoidably detained. Gianni will es-
cort you to my mother's house and I will see
you at the party this evening.
A dopo,
Marco

No kiss, she noted. What did that mean in a
time when even her dentist included an X on
her check-up reminder? Pocketing the note, she
smiled at Gianni. 'Thank you for coming to meet
me. I'm ready whenever you are.'

She'd spoken too soon. As she got her first
glimpse of Venice Sophie realised that nothing
could have prepared her for her first glimpse of
the magnificent island city. Gianni led her out
of the airport and, instead of heading to a car
park, Sophie found herself at a dock. 'This way,
please,' Gianni said, briskly walking her past
the ferry port and the queues for the water taxis.
Sophie wanted to stop and take in the strange

sight of passengers embarking onto a row of boats, swaying on the gangplanks as they tried to balance their suitcases. All around her, voices exclaimed, yelled and barked in a mixture of languages, the fresh salt smell of the sea mixing with the less romantic scent of diesel.

They walked on for another few minutes until Gianni gestured her forward onto a gangplank that led onto a gleaming wooden boat. Two seats at the front were shielded from the elements by a simple screen and a further three comfortable-looking leather benches were arranged around the walls of the small glassed-in cabin. Gianni heaved her suitcase and bag onto the cabin floor, but when he gestured for Sophie to step inside she shook her head. 'Oh, please, can I sit up front, next to you? I've never been to Venice before.'

Gianni cast an assessing look at her quilted coat and the black velvet jeans she'd chosen to travel in. '*Sì*, but it gets cold on the sea. Do you have a hat?'

'And a scarf and gloves,' Sophie assured him as she took her place beside the driver's seat—or pilot's seat. She wasn't entirely sure of the correct term for a boat driver.

It took just a few moments for Gianni to cast off the ropes and expertly manoeuvre the boat out of the dock and around the fleet of ferries, water taxis and hotel boats out into the lagoon. Sophie sucked in a breath of sheer exhilaration as the boat accelerated through the clear blue water and headed towards the most beautiful place she'd ever seen. The island city rose out of the water like a stately dame.

"'Age cannot wither her, nor custom stale her infinite variety",' Sophie quoted as the bell tower in St Mark's Square came into view. It seemed so familiar and yet so new—a picture she'd seen a thousand times and yet never really got until now. Sophie's heart squeezed and she knew she would always love this ancient city. It was in her blood already, taking further root with every breath.

She couldn't speak as Gianni steered the boat into the Grand Canal, just stared, almost overcome by the beauty all around her. Boats passed them, turning down narrow canals, bridges arched overhead and, glancing down a canal on her right, Sophie thrilled as she saw a boat piled high with a colourful variety of fruit and vegetables moored to the side, the owner twisting up produce in paper bags as he sold to eager customers.

It wasn't just the beauty of the city, it was the life thrumming through it. This was no museum, a place existing merely for the multitudes of tourists. It was a living, breathing place—and for the next two days she would be part of it. Would belong.

At that moment the boat began to turn and headed towards a small gangplank and a set of stairs leading directly to a door to an imposing cream-coloured building right on the Grand Canal. What was going on? She'd done a little research and knew that the hotels overlooking the famous canal were exorbitant. Sophie had expected a little B & B somewhere further out of the city. 'Wait, where are you going?'

Gianni looked puzzled. 'To Palazzo Santoro, of course. Signor Santoro asked me to convey you directly.'

'The *palazzo*?' Sophie's hands tightened on the side of the boat. Marco hadn't mentioned a *palazzo*—especially not one right on the Grand Canal. Her stomach twisted. Girls from the Manchester suburbs didn't belong in places like this—not unless they were serving drinks. She took a deep breath. *Palazzo* probably didn't mean anything grand. Maybe Marco's mother had a flat in this building. No one actually *owned* a building this big, no one Sophie was ever going to meet.

Before she could completely gather her thoughts the boat had stilled and Gianni was lifting her bags out of the back of the boat and extending a hand to help her disembark. Sophie climbed gingerly over the side of the boat and followed Gianni, treading carefully up the stone steps. He rapped smartly on the door and, as it opened, set Sophie's bags inside, gave her a friendly nod and ran lightly back down the steps and into the boat. She looked around wildly, hoping for a clue as to where exactly she was going, but all she could see was the open door. And her suitcase and travel bag were inside.

It fleetingly crossed Sophie's mind that no one knew exactly where she was—or who Marco was—and she could enter this house and never be seen again. But if it was a kidnap plot, it was far too elaborate a set-up for a waitress living on the outer edges of Chelsea. She took another step up the last step and entered through the ornately carved wooden door and came to an abrupt standstill.

Had she fallen down a rabbit hole? Sophie had cleaned and waitressed in some seriously swanky homes over the last year or so, but she had never seen anything quite on this scale or of this antiquity. The door led into an immense tiled hallway with a wooden-beamed ceiling and aged-looking frescos on the wall and ceiling, the only furnishings a few very old and very delicate-looking chairs. The hall ran the entire length of the building; she could see double doors at the other end, windows on either side, the sun streaming through the stained glass at the top. A gallery with intricate wrought-iron railings ran all the way around the hallway, accessed by two wide staircases, one at either end of the hall. Sophie could see several closed doors running the length of the room, discreetly hidden in the faded frescos.

What she couldn't see was any sign of life. She stepped further in, swivelling slowly as she took in every detail, jumping at the sight of the elderly woman, clad in sombre black from throat to calf, standing statuelike almost behind the open door. 'Oh, hello. I mean *buongiorno.*' All her hastily learned Italian phrases seemed to have disappeared from her head. *'Je m'appelle…* No, sorry, that's not right. Erm…*mi chiamo* Sophie. Marco is expecting me, isn't he? The driver, boatman, he seemed to think he was at the right place.'

That's right, Sophie, just keep babbling.

She was struck by a sudden thought: maybe this was a hotel and the Santoro was just a co-incidence—it could be a totally common name like Smith or Brown. 'Should I check in?' she enquired hopefully. A check-in desk she could cope with. House rules, room-service menu, hopefully a fluffy white robe.

The woman didn't respond. Instead she bent slowly, so slowly Sophie could almost hear the creak of her waist, before picking up Sophie's suitcase as if it weighed less than an empty pillowcase. Sophie, who had stepped forward to stop her, froze in place as the woman stepped forward, the suitcase almost swinging from her hand. It had taken all Sophie's efforts just to heave that suitcase onto the Tube. She eyed the woman with respect and stood back out of her way as the woman strode past her with a grunted 'This way' as she did so. Sophie followed meekly behind, along the hallway, up three flights of the sweeping staircase and onto a long landing peopled with portraits of men in tights and women with fans. Sophie was panting by this point, but the woman seemed completely at ease and Sophie yet again promised herself a regular routine of Pilates, Zumba and body pump.

They came to an abrupt halt outside a wood-panelled door. The woman pushed it open and gestured for Sophie to step inside. With a wondering glance she did so, her aching legs and heaving chest instantly forgotten as she turned around in wonder.

The room was huge, easily twice the size of

Sophie's entire apartment with three huge floor-to-ceiling windows overlooking the canal, shutters swung open to reveal the Juliet balconies outside each one, Venice framed like a living breathing picture within. Although the walls were painted a simple pale blue the ceiling was alive with a fresco of cherubs and angels, partying riotously across the room, edged in gilt matching the elaborate gilt headboard on the huge bed and the elegant chaise positioned before one of the windows. A huge mirror hung opposite the windows reflecting the watery light. The woman—a maid? Marco's grandmother? A complete stranger? Sophie had absolutely no idea—opened one of two matching doors on either side of the bed to reveal a dressing room, complete with dressing table and two wardrobes. The other door led into a bathroom so luxurious Sophie thought she might never be able to leave it.

'The family will gather in the reception room at six,' the lady intoned and left, shutting the door firmly behind her, leaving Sophie standing in the middle of the room torn between giddiness at the gorgeousness of her surroundings and fear at trying to find her way through this huge house to meet a set of people she didn't even have names for.

'Breathe,' she told herself. 'Live a lot, remember?' But as she sank onto the bed she was painfully conscious that all she wanted to do was hide away in this room.

Okay, here was what she knew: this was not an apartment; Marco's family appeared to own the entire, immense and very old building. Therefore the family party was unlikely to be just a few close friends, a glass of sherry and some pineapple and cheese sticks in the kitchen. The only person she knew was Marco and he wasn't even here and didn't expect to be until the party. She lay down and stared up at the cherubs, hoping they might be able to help her.

On the other hand she *was* in Venice. Sophie sat up and rolled off the bed, almost running to the window before the thought had fully formed, staring out with rapt eyes at the *palazzos* opposite, at the boats sailing below. She was in *Venice* and about to go to a party with a gorgeous man before returning to the most beautiful room she had ever set eyes on. So she was a little daunted? Time to pull on her big-girl pants—well, the nicest underwear she owned *just in case*—and try to enjoy every moment because she knew all too well that moments like this didn't come her way all too often.

'Come on, Sophie. Enjoy it. It's just a couple of days...' Two days of being someone new. Nobody here knew her, nobody here knew that she was twenty-six, had wasted the last eight years of her life, that she worked sixteen hours a day trying to pay her bills and get her own business off the ground. She wasn't Sophie Bradshaw, reliable employee of Maids in Chelsea, waitress, chambermaid and cleaner. She was Signorina Bradshaw, the kind of woman who went to glamorous balls and got invited to stay in *palazzos*. Why not be that woman for two days? After all, she wasn't expecting to see Marco again after she went back to London. What harm could it do to live the fantasy, just for a little while?

But as she turned to look back at the ornate room fear struck her once again. How would a girl like her ever fit in a place like this? Even if it was for just a couple of days?

Marco adjusted his bow tie, painfully aware that he was running almost inexcusably late. It had been a long six days. Since his move to London Marco had kept his visits back to Venice as brief as possible—he'd been confident in his contacts in Italy; it had been the rest of the world he'd needed to concentrate on. But a decade was a long time and it was becoming painfully clear a couple of days twice a year was no longer enough. He needed to start spending some significant amounts of time here if he wanted to continue to grow his business.

His mother was also making it very clear that it was time he stepped up and assumed his role as head of the family. Only, guided by her, of course... His mouth thinned. He'd already fought that battle with one parent and he wasn't sure either of them could count a decade-long standoff as a victory. And now his father was gone it all seemed pointlessly self-destructive anyway.

But how could he complain about the burden of his name when every now and then it opened doors to homes and estates that were kept firmly shut to less exalted sons of the city? Today he had spent the day with an impoverished old Venetian family who were reluctantly selling off some of their family treasures and trusted Marco to do the job for them both lucratively and discreetly. Neither would prove to be difficult; he had a long list of potential buyers who would pay more than market value for first refusal on the beautifully carved furniture, Renaissance paintings and elaborate silverware.

A negotiation like this took time and he had been all too aware that while he was sitting drinking coffee with the Grigionis and dancing ever so politely around his commission, Sophie had arrived to an empty house with nobody to welcome her but Marta, who was a most excellent woman but not the most gregarious of people—and the chances were very high that she would run into his mother before he could warn Sophie just what he was bringing her into.

Several times over the last few days he had

been on the verge of cancelling Sophie's visit. His mother had been so focussed on finding him a suitable Venetian bride he'd hoped Sophie's presence would throw her long enough to give him some space—but he'd underestimated her desire to see him wed. His father's death seemed to have intensified her hopes, and nationality no longer seemed to matter. His mother's eyes had lit up at the news he had invited a date to the party and she hadn't stopped asking him questions about his English 'friend'.

At least with Sophie by his side she wouldn't be able to introduce him to any eligible female guests with that specifically intense focus she usually employed. No, it was probably a good thing he hadn't cancelled. Sophie was here for just a couple of nights, not long enough for his mother to get too attached to her but long enough to throw her off the scent for the rest of his visit. Bringing a diversion was an excellent idea; he didn't know why he hadn't considered it earlier.

The clock had finished striking six when Marco strolled into the salon, adjusting his cuffs as he did so. Sophie was already there talking to his mother and his sister, Bianca, looking a little paler than he remembered but stunning in a pale pink beaded dress, which hung straight down to mid-thigh from two simple knotted straps. Her long blonde hair was knotted up with tendrils curling around her face, her only jewellery a pair of striking gold hoop earrings, which trembled as she moved. His blood began to pulse hot at the sight of her exposed neck. Inviting her had been an excellent idea for several reasons.

'Sophie,' he said, striding over to her and kissing her on both cheeks in welcome. 'Welcome. Did you have any trouble finding us?'

'No, no, even I would find it hard to get lost when a boat delivers me straight to the door.' Bianca and his mother laughed, but Marco's eyes narrowed. There was a tartness in her voice he hadn't heard before, the blue eyes icy and cold. Was she cross because he hadn't met her at the airport? He hoped not. Maybe a decoy was going to be as much trouble as a real girlfriend.

'Mamma, Bianca, please excuse us, I would like to make my apologies to Sophie properly for not being here when she arrived,' he said, smoothly drawing Sophie's arm through his. The pre-party drinks were being held in the reception salon, the largest sitting room on the first floor. Like most of the public rooms it overlooked the Grand Canal. Marco walked Sophie over to the furthest window, away from prying ears. 'I hope Gianni found you all right. I'm sorry I was detained.'

'No, that's fine.' But she was still staring out at the canal, her face set. 'I just wish you'd warned me, that's all.'

'I didn't realise until yesterday...'

'No! Not about being met, for goodness' sake! About this...' She looked around and he realised with a stab of compunction that her lips were quivering. 'Marco, every woman here is in a full-on ballgown. They look like they are going to a coronation, not a family party. And me? I'm wearing a little party dress I made myself. I look so underdressed.'

'You look beautiful.' And she did. Although she was right, all the other women were in floor-length, brightly coloured silk and chiffon gowns.

'And this house! Family party, you said. You

forgot to mention that the family is the Borgias! I've never been anywhere like this. My bedroom is like a five-star hotel.'

'You don't like it?' Marco was struggling to understand the point she was making. So the family home was big and the party formal? Women usually loved the *palazzo*, and they loved knowing he was the future owner—owner, he supposed, not that he had any intention of setting up home here even more.

'Like it?' She made a queer noise, part gasp, part sob, part laughter. 'It's not the kind of place you like, is it? It's magnificent, beautiful, incredible, but it's not the kind of place I know as home. I don't fit in here, Marco. Not in this house, not with this kind of wealth. Your mother is wearing a diamond tiara that's probably worth more than my parents' house.' She shook her head. 'Oh, God, listen to me. I sound like the worst kind of inverted snob. I just didn't expect any of this. I'm more than a little thrown.'

Marco had never heard this kind of reaction before. True, most women who walked into the *palazzo* knew exactly who he was, briefed by their *mammas* just as he was by his. But even the wealthiest and most well-bred visitor got a covetous look in their eye when they realised the whole of the building still belonged to the family and therefore, by extension, to Marco. This kind of appalled shock was new, but it was also a relief, like a long sip of cold water after a lifetime of rich, creamy milk.

And she did have a point. He'd brought her here for his own selfish reasons; it hadn't occurred to him to warn her just what a Santoro party entailed.

'Just be yourself, Sophie. I promise you, everyone will love you—and they will adore your dress. I'm sorry, it didn't occur to me that this would all be a little overwhelming, but I promise to make it up to you. Tomorrow I'll show you Venice, not a tiara in sight. What do you say?'

She didn't answer for a long moment, indecision clear on her face. Then she turned to him, eyes big with a vulnerable expression in them that struck him hard. 'Are you sure I look all right? I'm not letting you down?'

'Not at all,' he assured her. 'In fact I predict

next year most of the younger women will be glad to break with tradition and wear shorter dresses. Come, let's go and mingle and I will tell you three scandalous secrets about every person we meet. I promise you won't be intimidated by a single one by the end of the evening.'

CHAPTER FIVE

ALTHOUGH MARCO WAS true to his word and did indeed tell Sophie such scandalous secrets about every person she met—she refused to believe they could be true; *surely* that regal lady over there wasn't an international jewel thief?—she was still a little intimidated. Intimidated by the glitter and the air of self-possession displayed by every well-dressed guest, by the rapid flow of Italian all around and the familiarity with which each guest greeted each other. She felt too English, too parochial, too poor, too self-conscious, and although Marco was a charming and attentive host Sophie couldn't help thinking longingly of the city outside the old *palazzo*, ready to be explored and discovered.

But when Marco took her arm in his, when he leaned in close to whisper yet another outrageous lie, when he caught her eyes, laughter lurking in his, as his mother not so discreetly quizzed Sophie on her future plans and whether those plans involved marriage and babies, then she was pulled away from the room, away from her insecurities and into a world where all she saw was the tilt of his mouth, the warmth of his smile and the promise in his dark eyes. Anticipation flooded through her at the knowledge that when the clock struck twelve her night would only just be beginning... At least she hoped it would; she hadn't splashed out on a gorgeous new nightie in the New Year sales for nothing. The bits of silk held together with lace would hardly keep her warm after all.

She was aware of Marco's eyes on her and heat flooded through her as their gazes snagged and held, the rest of the room falling away. No, the other women in the room could do their best to attract his attention—and many of them were— but Sophie knew she wouldn't be sleeping alone that night.

After drinks and appetisers and a formal, beautifully presented meal for fifty, the party moved into an even grander and bigger room.

Here yet more guests joined them, the numbers swelling into the hundreds as a band played at one end and immaculately dressed waiters circled with trays of drinks. Marco's mother had 'borrowed' him to greet an elderly relative and Sophie hovered by the window, unsure where to go or who to speak to—if she could make herself understood, that was. It was all too reminiscent of standing at the back of one of Harry's gigs, not quite knowing what to say or whether she was welcome in any of the close-knit, self-possessed groups.

'I'm sorry, it must all be a little too much for you. We are bad enough when it's just the family, but when all of Venice is here? I wish I could run and hide, so I have no idea how horrifying you must find tonight.'

Sophie turned to see Marco's sister, Bianca, standing beside her, a sympathetic smile on her heart-shaped face. She was very beautiful in a classically Italian way with masses of dark wavy hair and huge brown eyes fringed with lashes so long they made Sophie gasp with envy, tall and shapely with a generous bosom spilling out of the top of her low-cut strapless dress.

'It's a little more than I was expecting. Marco didn't quite communicate the full scale of the evening. I didn't expect to meet so many people. As you can see I'm not really dressed appropriately...' She gestured towards her dress self-consciously, aware that the hand-sewn beads and cheap fabric paled beside Bianca's ravishing emerald silk gown.

'Your dress is *bellissima*,' Bianca reassured her. 'I have heard many envious comments. Of course, you have such lovely ivory skin. That pale pink would make me far too sallow. I predict next year half the younger women will break with convention and wear something a little more fun and fashionable.' Bianca echoed her brother's prediction.

'Thank you.' Sophie didn't think her skin looked lovely or ivory, more the pale blue an English winter turned her naturally pale complexion. She'd much rather be blessed with Bianca's gorgeous olive skin and generous curves.

'And the cut, I love how it is so modern and yet looks so vintage. Who's the designer?'

'Oh, well, I am.' Sophie always felt absurdly diffident when admitting to designing or making her clothes. Her friends were supportive, asking for commissions and nagging her into starting a website to sell to a wider audience, but they were her friends—it was their job to tell her to follow her heart and aim high. Showing her work to other people was exposing. Harry had always told her that she was wasting her time and the problem was she didn't only believe him then, she still half believed him now.

'You made this? But, Sophie, it is incredible. No wonder it fits you so well. You are so talented.'

'Thank you, but it's not that hard…'

'Of course it is! I can barely thread a needle. Do you make all your clothes?'

'Most of them,' Sophie admitted. 'Some from scratch, with new material, but many of my clothes are do-overs. I buy them from charity shops or in sales, tear them apart and put them back together again.'

'How creative.' Bianca sighed. 'I tried for years to find my talent, but no matter how many private lessons I had I remained tone deaf, turned into a plank of wood on stage, and I'm still incapable of drawing better than a five-year-old. Antonio tells me not to worry, that handling spreadsheets is a talent in itself, but I'd much rather be a dancer than an accountant.'

'You're an accountant?' Sophie always thought of accountants as faded and grey—not vibrant and full of life like the woman in front of her.

'Head of Finance at Antonio's company. It's how we met. He says marrying me will stop me being headhunted—I let him think that. I don't want to shatter his illusions! But I'd like to work for an international company if I get the opportunity. All those complicated tax laws would be really interesting.'

'Quite.' Sophie had no idea what to say, all her preconceptions tumbling down. It had been too easy to look at Bianca and see nothing but the beautifully dressed daughter of an obviously wealthy family—but there was clearly a lot more to her than that. 'As someone who can dance and sew but gets a cold sweat at the thought of a budget I have to say I think you got the better end of the deal.'

'Maybe. So where did you and Marco meet?'

Here it was. The interrogation. Sophie had already been through something similar from Marco's mother, an aunt and his godmother. 'At a party. Actually after the party, it was snowing and we sort of…collided.'

'How romantic.' The dark eyes were keen and focussed very intently on Sophie. 'Snow and an unexpected encounter. And you've seen much of each other since?'

'I wouldn't say much.' She forced a laugh. 'How friendly everyone is and they all want to know about me.'

'You must think we're all very nosy. But this is the first time in a long time that Marco has ever willingly brought a date to any occasion—and definitely the first time he brought someone Mamma hasn't set him up with. So you see, we are all consumed with curiosity to find out more about the mysterious English girl who has captured my brother's heart.'

Who had *what*? What exactly had Marco intimated? 'I wouldn't go that far. We are still getting to know each other. It's very early days...'

The two women had drifted over to one of the uncomfortable formal-looking sofas and Bianca sat down with a relieved 'Oomph, my feet are so swollen. How I am going to manage a whole wedding in heels, I don't know. I usually wear flats, I'm so tall. But Mamma insisted I wear heels on my wedding day. Luckily Antonio is tall too, so I won't tower over him!'

'You're getting married soon?' Really, it was absurd how ill prepared she was to meet this family. Next time a gorgeous stranger suggested a spontaneous trip to a family party she would insist on crib sheets and a written exam first.

'Next week.' Bianca sighed. 'Only, I think I ate too much over Christmas and I'm really scared my dress won't do up. The shame! But look at the size of my breasts! I'm going to be falling out of it, I know it.'

'But you must have a final fitting booked, surely? There will be something they can do. Let out a seam or fit a false back. I wouldn't worry, a good designer is always prepared for some fluctuation in weight.'

'But she's not here. She's gone to New Zealand for the whole month and won't be back until after the wedding. I didn't think it would be a problem. My weight doesn't usually change...' Bianca's voice trailed off and she looked so woebegone Sophie couldn't help sympathising.

'I could take a look,' she suggested. 'Make a few suggestions. Obviously it depends on the fabric and cut, but I might be able to help.' As soon as she said the words she wanted to snatch them back. What was she thinking? A wedding dress? A designer wedding dress no doubt, costing thousands and made of the best silks and laces. As if she were qualified to do as much as tack a hem on that kind of gown, let alone attempt some kind of alteration, but, Sophie realised with a sinking heart, it was too late to backtrack. Bianca was clutching at her arm, gratitude beaming out of her eyes.

'Really? You'd do that?'

'Well...I...'

'Oh, Sophie, that's so wonderful. *Grazie.* It's

such a relief to know that you're right here. Wait, when are you going back to London?'

'The day after tomorrow, but I'm sure I can find time to look at it before I go, make some suggestions.'

'The day after tomorrow? But the wedding isn't for another week! What if something else changes?'

Sophie's smile froze. She'd heard tales of bridezillas but had never had to deal with one before, not even at work. In fact Emma's vow renewal was the first time she'd been directly involved with the bridal party, not a duty invite or a plus-one on the guest list—somehow she'd let her few school friends slip away through the Harry years and had never really connected with his friends' ever-changing parade of girlfriends.

'I'm sure it will be fine…'

But Bianca was shaking her head. 'So much could go wrong—a button could loosen or a hem fray or my veil need adjusting. What was I thinking to choose a designer who isn't here for the wedding? It has to be perfect. But if you were here, I wouldn't have to worry.'

'Bianca, no one would notice if a button was loose, I promise.'

'And what if I get bigger? Or smaller? With all the stress, I don't know if I'll lose my appetite or eat chocolate for the next seven days. Everything is very unpredictable at the moment.' To Sophie's horror Bianca's voice began to waver. She wasn't going to cry on her, was she?

'It's only a week. I'm sure it won't make any difference if you eat nothing but chocolate, not at this stage.'

'And this is your first time in Venice, no? You can't possibly see the city in just one day. Marco should have known better. You must stay, see the city properly and then come to the wedding. I would love to have you.' She turned to Sophie, her smile wide again, all traces of tears miraculously disappeared. 'There, now we are all happy, me, you and Marco. Perfect.'

'What will make me happy?'

Sophie's stomach turned as Marco strode up beside them. He'd think she'd been plotting with his sister, think the *palazzo* had turned her head and she wanted to stay, to inveigle her way into his family.

'Nothing. Bianca is panicking a little about her wedding, but I'm telling her not to worry,' she said quickly.

He raised an eyebrow. 'Don't tell me, the flowers are out of season and so you need to call the whole wedding off? She used to be quite sensible,' he added to Sophie, 'until this wedding nonsense.'

'It's not nonsense. Wait until it's your turn,' Bianca said indignantly. 'But, Marco, wait. I have a wonderful idea. Sophie should stay here with us until the wedding and come as your date. What do you think?'

Sophie should *what*? Marco froze to the spot, eyes narrowed at his beaming sister. Had she been consulting with their mother? Was this some elaborate plot? Was Sophie in on it? He cast her a quick glance. No, her cheeks were red and eyes lowered in mortification.

'What do I think?' he repeated.

'He thinks it's impossible.' Sophie reached up

and took his hand, giving it a reassuring squeeze. 'I have to get back and he doesn't need a date anyway. I don't want to cramp his style.'

'Nonsense,' Bianca said. 'He would love to have you there.'

Amusing as it was to hear the two women politely disagree about what he did or didn't want, it was time to take control. 'Of course I would love to have you attend the wedding with me, Sophie, but if you have to get back, then there is no more to say. Besides, I have a lot to do over the next few days and I would hate you to be bored here alone.'

Bianca shot to her feet and glared at him. 'It's my wedding and I want her there. I need her, Marco.'

'But…' He wasn't often at a loss for words, but seeing his usually sensible, logical sister so het up robbed him of all coherent speech. 'Bianca, Sophie's said she needs to get back. You can't force her to stay.'

But as he said the words he began to consider just what would happen if Sophie *did* stay. He'd warned her he had to work so there would be no expectation for him to be responsible for her—and then when they returned to England he'd give it a few weeks before casually telling his mother they had parted company. In the meantime… He laced his fingers through hers, enjoying the smoothness of her skin against his. In the meantime it had been too long since he had enjoyed one of his discreet affairs. Two nights and a day wasn't long enough, not when every time she moved the beads on her dress shimmered, showcasing the outline of her breasts, the shapeliness of her calves.

And she'd made it very clear to him she wasn't interested in anything long-term…

'Of course, if there was some way you could arrange things so that you could spend a few more days with us, then you would be very welcome, Sophie.' He smiled at her. 'Besides, bitter experience has taught me that Bianca usually gets her way, so it saves time if you just agree with her at the start.'

'But…you don't want, I mean, this is a family occasion.'

'Three hundred guests, at least a hundred of

whom are my parents' business associates and another hundred Bianca and Antonio's clients. I wouldn't worry about gatecrashing.'

Her mouth opened and she stared at Bianca incredulously. 'Three hundred guests?'

'You see why it has to be perfect? Please, Sophie, say yes. I'll be in your debt for ever.'

Marco knew not many people were able to resist Bianca when she turned the full force of her charm on them and Sophie was no different. 'I suppose I could take a few more days off work. I have a lot of holidays saved up. I'm not a miracle worker,' she warned his sister, 'but I'll do my best. Okay, if you really want me to, I'll stay, but, honestly, you might be better off consulting a professional.'

'I am so happy.' Bianca clapped her hands. 'When can you take a look? Tomorrow?'

It was time to intervene. 'Tomorrow, Bianca, Sophie belongs to me. You can have her the rest of the week. No...' as she tried to interrupt '... you need to practice patience, my child. Sophie, there's someone over here I would like to introduce you to. Bianca has been monopolising you long enough.' He pulled Sophie to her feet, giving his pouting sister a mock bow. '*Arrivederci*, Bianca.'

'Who are you introducing me to?' Sophie asked as he walked her away from the party, opening a door hidden in the ballroom panelling and ushering her into the small adjoining salon, lit only by a few low lamps. 'I hate to break it to you, but the party is that way and there's no one here. Unless it's some ancestor of yours,' she added, looking up at the huge portraits hanging over the mantelpiece. 'He doesn't look overly impressed with your choice of date.'

'That's my great, great, many more greats grandfather Lorenzo Santoro. He didn't approve of anyone or anything by all accounts, a problem in pleasure-loving Venice.'

'I won't take it personally, then.' She turned and faced him, her hair gleaming gold in the low lights, the dress swaying seductively around her thighs. 'So if you don't want to introduce me to Lorenzo, then who am I here to meet?'

'Me. I haven't seen you since New Year's Eve, almost a week ago, and I've neglected you shamefully since you got here. I think it's time I made amends.' He noted with some satisfaction how her colour rose at his words, tinging her cheeks, throat and décolletage a delicate rose pink.

'Oh…' She looked up at him then, the blue eyes earnest. 'Marco, it was really nice of you to ask me here in the first place. I'd really hate for you to think I was trying to force you into extending my invitation. Your sister seems so worried about her dress, I offered to help and the next thing I knew…'

'Sophie, I know exactly what my sister is like, please don't worry. If you wish to stay for the wedding, then I would love for you to do so, but if she railroaded you…'

'She did, but it's not exactly a hardship to stay here and explore Venice a bit more.'

'Then it's settled, you stay. And, Sophie?'

'Yes?'

He took a step closer. 'Let's get one thing straight. I wasn't being nice when I asked you here.'

'You weren't?'

'Not at all. I wanted to see you again.' His gaze dropped to her full mouth. 'I wanted to renew our acquaintance.'

'To renew our acquaintance?' she echoed. 'So that's what they call it nowadays.'

Another step. 'Do you know what this room is?'

That elusive, kissable dimple peeked out at the corner of her mouth. 'Another room for unsuspecting guests to get lost in?'

'Did you see how the door was almost hidden in the panelling? It's an assignation room. Ancestors would slip away in the middle of a ball to meet their lovers here discreetly.'

'Not Grandfather Lorenzo surely?'

'Probably not him. But the rest of the Santoros. We're a degenerate lot.'

'Consider me warned. So, Signor Santoro, did you bring me here for nefarious purposes?'

His voice was soft but full of intent and satisfaction ran through him as he saw her shiver, her eyes dilating at his words. 'I wanted to say hello to you properly.'

'And how were you planning to do that?'

She was teasing him, leading him exactly where she wanted him to go, exactly where he wanted to be. Here, now, no need to plan or think ahead. Just two people enjoying all the benefits of mutual attraction. He took another step and then another, backing her up until she hit the wall, her breath coming in short pants. Slowly but with absolute intent Marco put one arm on the wall and leaned in so she had to look up at him, her body guarded by his, surrounded by his. It took all his strength not to pull her in close, crush her against him, not to lose himself in that mouth, that small perfect body, her sweet-smelling hair. 'Hello.'

'Hi yourself.'

Her mouth curved, the dimple provoking him, daring him, tempting him and, with a groan, he succumbed, dipping his tongue into the small hollow, her answering shiver pushing the last restraints away. With a smothered growl he swung her up in his arms, capturing her mouth with his, inhaling, demanding, needing, taking as he carried her over to the chaise, discreet in the corner of the room. Her kiss was equally fierce, her hands twisted in his hair as he lowered her onto the green brocade. Sophie lay, hair fanned out around her, eyes half closed, chest heaving. Marco stared down at her, trying to regain some vestiges of control. She extended a hand, her eyes wicked in the lamplight. 'Come on, then, *signor*, show me just how a Santoro conducts an illicit liaison.'

CHAPTER SIX

'GOOD MORNING, SLEEPYHEAD.' Marco looked up as Sophie entered the ridiculously huge breakfast room. He looked completely at home—not surprising, she reminded herself. This *was* his home. He sat back in a comfortable-looking chair, newspaper spread open before him on the polished table, coffee in one hand. It was all quite normal—or at least it would be if the table weren't large enough to seat thirty, every chair an antique and the view out of the line of shuttered windows not one she had seen in a hundred iconic photos.

'It's only eight a.m.—and considering I'm still on London time and got lost three times finding the breakfast room…' Was this whole room seriously just to eat breakfast in? It was plausible. The *palazzo* was big enough to have a brunch room, afternoon-tea room, supper room and midnight-snack room if the owners wished. 'I think I'm pretty bright and early.'

Especially as the man lounging opposite with a wicked grin in his eyes had kept her up half the night, leaving her room sometime in the early hours. It was better to be discreet, he'd said; his mother would be calling the banns if she found him in there—but Sophie hadn't minded. Sex was one thing, it was just intense chemistry, but sleeping together? That was real intimacy.

Marco smiled, the slow, sexy grin that made the breath leave her lungs and her knees weaken. 'I thought we'd get breakfast out, the Venetian way. Are you ready to go or do you need more time?'

'Ready? I've been ready since you mentioned this trip, ready since I got a passport, since I first saw Indiana Jones. I mean, we have canals in Manchester, but it's not quite the same. And the sun's shining. In January! What else could I possibly need?' Sophie had dressed with care for a day's sightseeing in a grey wool dress she had bought from a Chelsea charity shop and then redesigned, taking it in, shortening it and adding pink and purple flower buttons in two vertical rows to the flared skirt. A pair of black-and-grey-striped tights, her comfiest black patent brogues, her thick black jacket and a bright pink hat and gloves completed her outfit. She bounced on her toes. 'Let's go.'

Marco took a last, deliberate swig of his coffee before pushing his chair back and languidly getting to his feet. 'In that case, *signorina*, I'm at your service. I thought we'd start the day on foot and head onto the water later. Does that sound agreeable?'

'On foot. By boat, or even on a donkey. I'm happy any way you choose.'

Sophie had been too anxious the day before to really take Venice in. She had clear flashes of the city like snapshots of memory: the first glimpse of the Grand Canal, the flaking pastel paint on the canal-side *palazzos*, a gondola, boats crammed with people pulling in at a stop as nonchalantly as a red London bus stopping outside her flat. The greengrocer boat bartering and trading just like a market stall at the Portobello Market and yet strange and exotic. But the whole had escaped her and she was at fever pitch as Marco guided her along the gallery and down the stately staircase back into the vast hallway. It was almost an anticlimax when Marco ushered her out of the *palazzo's* grand double doors, at the other end of the hallway from the water door she had entered by, to find herself on a street, no water to be seen.

Okay, it was as far from her busy, traffic-filled, bustling London home as a street could be. Narrow and flagstoned, almost an alley, with aged buildings rising on either side. Doors lined up on both sides, some preceded by a step, others opening directly onto the street, and shuttered windows punctuated the plaster and stone of the graceful buildings. Voices floated from open windows, the Italian fast and incomprehensible. The air throbbed with vibrancy and life.

She hadn't expected this somehow. Venice was a fairy-tale setting, a film backdrop, a picture; she had forgotten it was a home too. How could Marco bear to live away from this unique beauty?

'This way,' he said, slipping on a pair of sunglasses against the sun's glare. He was more casually dressed than she had seen him so far in a pair of faded jeans, which clung perfectly in all the right places, a thin grey woollen jumper and a double-breasted black jacket. Somehow he managed to look both relaxed and elegant, a combination few British men could pull off. 'Hungry?'

'A little,' she admitted. 'Actually a lot. I could barely eat anything last night.' Nor had she managed much in the day, her stomach twisting with nerves.

'We don't usually have much for breakfast in Venice,' he said to her dismay. 'A coffee, maybe a brioche or small pastry standing up at the bar. But on a special occasion we visit a *pasticceria* for something a little more substantial. You do have a sweet tooth, don't you?'

Obviously it was far more sophisticated to say no, actually she only liked to nibble on raw cacao and a few olives were more than enough to satisfy her snack cravings, but honesty won out. 'Like a child in a sweet shop.'

'*Bene*, then I think you'll be more than happy.'

The next few hours slipped by like a dream. First Marco took her to a little neighbourhood *pasticceria*, which showcased a breathtaking array of little pastries and cakes in the display cabinets under the glass and wood counters. People dressed for work queued at the long polished wooden bar, where they quickly tossed back a small, bitter-looking coffee and maybe ate a pastry before ducking back out into the street, another caffeine seeker seamlessly moving into their place. Breakfast almost on the go. Marco and Sophie elected to take a little more time and sat at one of the elegant round tables, where Marco introduced Sophie to *frittelle*, round, doughnut-style pastries stuffed with pine nuts and raisins. 'They are usually eaten during *carnivale*,' he explained as Sophie uttered a moan of sheer delight at the taste. 'But some places make them all year round.'

'I'd love to see *carnivale*,' she said, licking her fingers, not wanting to waste even the tiniest crumb. 'It sounds so exotic.'

'It's crowded, noisy—and utterly magical. I have missed the last few, thanks to work, and every year I wish I'd been able to make the time to be here. There's nothing like it.'

Her curiosity was piqued by the longing in his voice. 'But you could live here if you wanted, couldn't you? You were working yesterday. Couldn't your business be based here?'

'Like I said in London, Venice is a village on an island. There's no escape. Besides, it's good to try somewhere new, you know that. Where are you from? Manchester, didn't you say? You moved cities too.'

He was eyeing her keenly and Sophie shifted, not comfortable with the conversation turning to her and her decision to move to London. 'I think every home town can feel like a village at times. So, what else are we going to do today and will it involve more cake?'

After their brief but sugar-filled breakfast Marco led her along some more twisty streets. At the end of every junction she could see water, her throat swelling with excitement every time she heard the swish of waves lapping against stone, until finally she was walking along a pavement bordering not a road, but a broad canal complete with boats; private boats, taxis, even a police boat serenely cruising along. Sophie had to stop and photograph everything, much to Marco's amusement—especially the fat ginger cat sunning himself on one of the wooden jetties.

She was especially charmed when their route brought them out at a *traghetto* pier and Marco, after a quick conversation and handshake, gestured for her to get in and stand in the long, narrow boat. Two more passengers joined them before the two oarsmen—one at the front and one at the rear—pushed off and began to steer the boat across the Grand Canal.

'These are the traditional way to cross the Grand Canal.' Marco was standing just behind her, one hand on her shoulder, steadying her as the boat rocked in the slight swell of the water. 'There are seven crossings, although there were many more when my parents were small. The businesses have often been in families for generations, passed on from father to son.'

'Why are there two prices? Is one a return?'

'One for tourists and one for residents, but Angelo here considered you a resident this time.'

'Because I'm with you?'

'And because he said you have beautiful eyes.'

Sophie could feel her cheeks heat up and she was glad Angelo was too busy rowing to notice her reaction—and that Marco couldn't see her face at all.

After disembarking from the *traghetto* they headed to the tourist mecca of St Mark's square. It was still too early for many visitors to be out and about—and now that the Christmas holidays were finished Venice was entering its quiet season—but they were far from alone in the vast space. People were taking photos of the ubiquitous pigeons and the imposing tower or were sitting outside one of the many cafés that lined the famous *piazza*. Sophie's camera was in her hand instantly, every view, every angle needing capturing whether it was the blue of the canal and the lagoon beyond or the old palace, dominating the other end of the square.

Three hours later Sophie was light-headed and slightly nauseous. They had toured the Doge's Palace, crossed the infamous Bridge of Sighs and, thanks to an old school friend of Marco's, got a chance to see some of the hidden parts of the palace including the *pozzi*, tiny, dank, dark cells where Casanova had once been imprisoned. When Marco suggested a walk down to the Rialto Bridge she gave him a pleading smile. 'Can I have some lunch first? I know it's early, but I'm hungry and my legs don't seem to want to walk anywhere without sustenance and a sit down.'

'*Sì*, of course.' He didn't seem at all put out that she hadn't fallen in with his suggestion. It was so refreshing; she'd never been able to make off-the-cuff suggestions to Harry. At the merest hint that his itinerary didn't suit her he would fall into a monumental sulk, which would need all her best cajoling and coaxing to pull him out of. Her heart clenched at the thought. What had she been thinking of? To allow such a spoilt brat to dictate her life for so long? Of all the ways to choose to assert her independence. If she could only go back in time and talk sense into her eighteen-year-old self, then…eighteen-year-old Sophie would probably have ignored her as she'd ignored everyone else. Too giddy with lust, with independence, too convinced it was love. Too foolish.

But no, she wasn't going to sully one moment of this perfect day thinking about her past, indulging in regrets. She was in Venice with a gorgeous, attentive man and he was about to provide lunch. Life really didn't get much better than that.

Marco knew the perfect place for lunch. Close enough to St Mark's for his hungry companion, far enough away to avoid tourist prices and menus. A locals' café, with fresh food, a menu that changed daily depending on what was in at the markets and a bustling, friendly atmosphere. He used to eat there with his father, but when long, conversational lunches had turned into lectures with food he had stopped coming. He couldn't wipe out the last ten years of cold civility, couldn't repair his father's heart—but maybe he could reclaim some of the spaces they used to inhabit.

They had barely set foot over the threshold when he saw her, straight-backed, elegant and as lethal as a tiger eyeing her prey. His chest tightened. She hadn't come in here to wait for them, had she? Surely even his mother wasn't that conniving. But it was barely noon and she usually ate a little later than this. And that was an unusually triumphant look in her eyes.

'Marco, *vita mia*, how lovely to see you and your *bella* friend.' She leant in and embraced Sophie, who returned the traditional two kisses with a dumbstruck look Marco was sure must be mirrored on his own face.

'Mamma,' he said drily. 'What a coincidence.'

'*Sì,*' she agreed, but even though her eyes were wide and candid, Marco knew better. 'But a lovely one, no? I barely got to talk to Sophie yesterday. I hear you are staying for Bianca's wedding? We are delighted to have you with us for longer and, Sophie, *cara*, please consider the *palazzo* your home the whole time you are in Venice.'

There was no way out. Half amused, half annoyed, Marco accepted his mother's invitation to join her and they were soon seated at an intimate table for three so his mother could begin her interrogation. At least the food would be good, he thought as he ordered a *vermicelli al nero di seppia* for himself, a dish he refused to eat anywhere other than Venice, and advised Sophie, who still looked a little pale, to try the risotto. He then poured them all a glass of the local Soave and sat back to watch the show.

'So, Sophie, what is it you do in London?' And she was off… If Sophie had any secrets, they would be expertly extracted before the bread and oil reached the table.

Or not. By the end of the meal Marco knew very little more than he had at the start. Maybe she was secret-service trained because Sophie Bradshaw had avoided every one of his mother's expertly laid traps like a professional—and what was more, she had done it in such a way Marco doubted his mother had noticed. She had mentioned two brothers and nieces and nephews—and then, while his mother had gone misty-eyed at the very thought of babies and grandchildren, had turned the tables and asked his mother so many questions about Bianca's forthcoming wedding his mother had been quite disarmed. Very clever.

Marco leaned back in his chair and eyed Sophie thoughtfully. It hadn't mattered that he knew little more than her name when she had been due to spend less than forty-eight hours with him, but now she was staying with his dangerously excitable family for over a week he found himself a little more curious. Who was Sophie Bradshaw and what did she really want? Was she really as happy with a casual relationship as she'd made out? She liked fashion and designing—although she had told his mother that she took other jobs while she worked to get her business off the ground. What other jobs? She came from Manchester but at some unspecified point had moved to London. She had two brothers and five nieces and nephews. That was it. All he knew.

He didn't need to know more. Why would he? After next week he would probably never see her again. But he'd never met a woman less willing to share—and there was a shadow behind those blue eyes that made him suspect there was a reason she was so reticent.

Whatever the reason, it was her business; he didn't need to get involved. Once you got involved, then expectations got raised, then things got messy. He knew that all too well.

It was with some amusement that Marco watched his mother kiss Sophie on both cheeks and embrace her warmly as they left the restaurant—and even more amusement that he heard Sophie suck in a huge sigh of relief. 'Well done, you held her off beautifully.'

'I thought I was going to crack any minute.'

'It was a good move to bring up Bianca's wedding. That's been her sole focus for the last year and the only thing guaranteed to distract her.'

'It nearly backfired though.' Sophie pulled on her gloves as they emerged into the bright, sunny but cold street. 'She managed to bring every question back to me. Would I prefer an A-line or a fitted dress, didn't I agree that an heirloom tiara was classier than a newly bought one, what colour scheme did I like, would I prefer a princess cut or a pear shape or maybe I wanted sapphires to match my eyes? I got the impression if I gave a straight answer to any question I'd have a ring on my finger and find myself frog-marched down an aisle whether I wanted to be or not.'

Her tone was light, but her words still struck him. He'd expected his mother to take an over-active interest in Sophie, but it was frustrating to have it confirmed that nothing had really changed, that ten years of exile, all the drama and anger had been for nothing. His mother had no intention of respecting his decisions. He tried to keep his own voice equally light, not to let his anger show. 'You can see why I asked you here. Mamma is obsessed with weddings. While she thinks there's a chance we might end up together she won't be busy matchmaking. It's perfect. I owe you, Sophie. Thank you.'

There was just the most infinitesimal pause before Sophie echoed, 'Yes, perfect. As long as I don't crack. Don't leave me alone with her, that's all I'm saying. I'm not sure I'd win in a straight duel. Has she always been this way?'

Marco began to stroll down towards the Rialto

Bridge. He planned for them to cross over the famous bridge and then head back to the *palazzo* to collect his boat for the afternoon. 'As long as I can remember.'

'But why? It's usually the other way round, isn't it? Pressure on the daughter to marry? I'm sure you're a catch and all...' The dimple was out again and he couldn't stop smiling back in response even though his mother's obsession with his future was his least favourite topic. And it wasn't easy to put into words.

'It's not about me, not really. She's obsessed with the past, the future, the *palazzo*. Venice is changing, has been for the last fifty years. More and more real estate is owned by foreigners, many of whom don't live here, which means more and more families moving onto the mainland. Both my parents came from ancient Venetian families, together they owned a lot of real estate, a lot of businesses around the city.' He allowed himself a brief smile. 'We're a city of traders, of merchants. Even I, though I wanted to set out on my own, trade goods back and forth. It's in my blood, like the sea.'

'What does that have to do with marriage?'

'It's about not letting the old bloodlines die out, with keeping a Santoro in the *palazzo*, running the family business, sons at his knees, just like the old days. Now Bianca is getting married—and to another scion of an ancient family—her attentions can be fully focussed on me. London might not be far enough. I may try Mars.'

'Would it be so bad? Marriage?' She held her hands up, laughing as he turned to look at her. 'That's not a proposal, by the way, not even a leading question. Just plain curiosity.'

'I'm the Santoro heir,' he said. 'It's a position that comes with privilege, sure, but also with expectations. I'm the only son. And from the moment I was born I was reminded that I had a duty to the family, to the name, to Venice. That what I want doesn't matter, that to pursue my dreams is a selfishness unbefitting a Santoro.' He could hear his father shouting the words as he spoke them. 'Marriage is part of that responsibility. So to me it isn't something natural, something healthy, something good. It's a heavy expectation I'm expected to bear. And now my father is gone…' He swallowed as he said the words. It still didn't seem possible. Venice seemed emptier without him, the *palazzo* hollower. 'Now I'm not just the only son, I'm the only remaining male, it's become even more imperative to my mother that I marry and soon. But the more she pushes, the less ready I feel. And I love my city, my family, of course I do. But I won't sacrifice myself, my integrity to tradition.'

'Have you told her?' Sophie asked softly. 'Told her how you feel. That you're not ready.'

His mouth quirked into a smile; if only it were that easy. 'Many times. But she only listens when she wants to. Hears what she wants to hear.'

'It's not good to let misunderstandings grow, let resentments fester.' There was a quiet certainty in Sophie's voice.

'I think we understand Mamma too well, Bianca and I. She was orphaned young, raised alone by her grandparents in an old *palazzo*. They had a title, an illustrious ancestry but no wealth. When she married my father she wanted security and a large family. Together they built up an empire to rival that of the early Santoros, but they had to settle for a small family. After Bianca she just couldn't conceive again. So she turned her attentions to grandchildren, to building the dynasty she always dreamed of. She thinks she knows best what will make us happy. I don't hurt her on purpose, but we have such different ideas on the way I should live.'

Hurt was inevitable. Every time he said 'no'. Every time he chose his own path. But if he didn't, then what had it all been for? The hard-fought-for independence, the ten years of estrangement, the knowledge he would never make it up with his father.

The knowledge that his father might even yet have been here, still alive, if Marco had been a different kind of man. More pliable, obedient.

'So you live in a different country and seldom come home?' Sophie was shaking her head. 'I don't know, Marco, it's a solution, but it doesn't sound like a good one. Not at all.'

And the worst thing was, Marco knew she was right. But what other choice did he have?

CHAPTER SEVEN

'DID YOU AND Marco have a good day yesterday?' Bianca's eyes were sly as she looked at Sophie in the mirror. 'Mamma was disappointed you didn't come back for supper. She was so looking forward to getting to know you better.'

Sophie circled Bianca, checking every seam and every hem. The dress was gorgeous, far bigger and more ornate than she would have chosen personally but perfect for a wedding as imposing as Bianca's promised to be. But Bianca's new curves spilled out of the silk ballgown's sweetheart neckline, turning it from daring to borderline indecent, and it was a struggle to get the zip up at the low back—in fact Sophie had decided against forcing it, not wanting to snag the delicate fabric.

'Lovely, thanks. We spent the morning at the palace, and then we had lunch with your mother, so I hope she wasn't too disappointed we missed supper, and then Marco took me out onto the lagoon for the afternoon.' He'd pointed out some of the more notable islands, promising to bring her back to visit one or two before the end of their trip, and then he had taken her to dine at an island hotel. Sailing in through the private water gate to be escorted up to the glassed-in terrace with views across to Venice itself had been the most romantic thing Sophie had ever experienced. If only she hadn't felt so tired and her appetite hadn't been so capricious. And if only she hadn't replayed Marco's words over and over in her mind. *You can see why I asked you here.*

She wasn't sure why those words had pricked her. She had been under no illusions about his sudden invitation; Marco hadn't brought her here because he'd been struck down with instalove—and she'd accepted for that very reason. But to have him spell out so baldly that she was a mere ploy to keep his mother happy was a little bruising to her pride.

But then again, after one lunch with his mother she fully accepted his reasons, sympathised with them even. Only, it would be nice to be more than convenient, to really matter to someone... She stopped still, staring down at Bianca's elaborate train. Where had that thought come from? She was happy on her own, remember? Not at all interested in a relationship.

But maybe one day. If she chose better, found someone who valued and cherished her the way her friends were loved and cherished, then maybe she could take that risk. Because if she did spend her life hiding from the possibility of love, did spend her life thinking she wasn't good enough, then Harry won after all, didn't he?

'Right.' Sophie blinked back unexpected, hot tears. What on earth was wrong with her? It was time to remember why she was here and not on a plane back to London. 'There's no way this dress is going to fit the way it is. Luckily your hips and waist have only increased by the smallest amount, so it's a reasonably easy fix, no major restructuring needed, but we do need to do something about the neckline.' She hesitated, searching for the right words. 'I could re-bone the bodice, but I still think you'll look more top-heavy than you intended. So what I'm proposing is that in addition to letting out the seams and adjusting the zip I make you a lace overdress. It's up to you if you just want it for your top or to cover the skirt as well. Look, I'll show you.' She picked up a gossamer-thin scarf and deftly twisted it around Bianca, pinning it in place.

'You need to imagine this is lace,' she warned Bianca. 'This is just to give us an idea.'

Sophie stepped back and pursed her lips as she fixed her design in her head. 'The beading on your skirt is lovely. It would be a real shame to cover it up with lace,' she decided. 'Let's go with a lace bodice. I'll find buttons to match your beads, tiny ones, and it can button up your back.' She shot Bianca a reassuring smile. 'I'll sew those on at the very last minute to make absolutely sure it fits.'

Bianca stared at herself in the mirror, hope flaring in her expressive dark eyes. 'Will it really work?'

'Absolutely.' In fact the more Sophie thought about it, the surer she was. 'I think it will be stunning. I can give you capped sleeves, little straps just off the shoulder—or we could go really regal with full-length sleeves, so decide what you'd prefer. The most important thing is making sure the lace matches the exact colour of the dress. Not all ivories are created equal. Do you have a swatch I can use?'

Bianca nodded, her eyes bright with tears. 'Thank you, Sophie. I can't begin to tell you how much I appreciate this, how much it means that you haven't just fixed my problem but made my dress even better.' She caught a tear with her finger, wiping it away, pulling a watery smile as she did so. 'If there is anything I can do to repay you...'

'No repayment necessary, I promise. I'm happy to do it. Let's get you out of the dress before you spoil the silk with your tears and I'll take a look at the zip. It only needs a few millimetres, I think, to be comfortable. I might not even need to add an insert. Unpicking the stitches and redoing it might be enough.'

It took a few minutes to manoeuvre Bianca out of the many folds of the dress, but eventually Sophie hung the layers of net and tulle and silk back up, smoothing the silk out with careful hands as she figured out the best way to deal with it. 'I wonder if I could get my hands on a tailor's dummy,' she pondered. 'If I put a dummy on a dais, I would find it easier. There must be somewhere I could source that from. I'll draw up a list of all we need: lace, silk, thread, buttons.'

'*Sì*, none of that should be a problem. The best place for lace is Burano, one of the islands. I'll ask Marco to take you. It's very pretty. I think you'll like it.'

'Sounds perfect.' Sophie turned to look at Bianca. The Italian girl sat on her unmade bed, a robe loosely drawn around her, the magnificent mane of hair spilling around her shoulders, tears still shimmering in her eyes.

'I'm sorry, Sophie, I'm not usually such a mess. The thing is…' she took a deep breath '…I didn't eat too much over Christmas, nor am I that stressed about the wedding, not really. It's just that…I'm having a baby and I haven't told anyone yet.'

'You're what? But that's wonderful. No wonder you've gone up over two cup sizes and barely gained a centimetre around your waist! How far along are you?'

'The doctor says ten weeks. I only realised at the end of last week. I've always been irregular, so I didn't notice any changes there, but I was always crying, or suddenly really hungry and then really nauseous. I've been so tired, light-headed. And I can't even cope with the smell of coffee, let alone the taste. Honestly, for someone with so many qualifications I can be very stupid, but I just didn't realise what was wrong. It wasn't like we were trying.'

Sophie perched onto the bed next to Bianca and patted her arm a little awkwardly. 'But this is good news, surely? After all, you're about to get married.'

'*Sì*, it is, at least, it will be, when I get used to it. I just thought we'd have time to *be* married before starting a family.'

'So,' Sophie asked gently, 'why the secrecy?'

'Antonio is stressed about the wedding, it's so big, I just don't want to give him anything else to worry about. I will tell him,' she said defensively as Sophie raised her eyebrows. 'I was planning to tonight—telling you was the first time I've said it out loud. It wasn't as hard as I expected.'

'And your mother will be over the moon.'

Bianca's mouth twisted. 'Oh, *sì*, Mamma will be delighted. But I won't be telling her until after the honeymoon. She can be a little overpowering.' She giggled. 'Okay, a lot overpowering. She already tried to take over the planning of the wedding, make it into her dream wedding, not mine. I'm not ready for her to take over the baby as well, not until I know how I feel about it all.'

'That makes sense.' But Sophie's mind had wandered back to something Bianca had said earlier. Something about not noticing that she was pregnant because she was irregular. Sophie was the complete opposite. In fact she was like clockwork, every twenty-eight days. Usually…

Frantically she counted back. Almost five weeks had passed since she had spent the night with Marco. Over five weeks without her period. Her regular-as-clockwork period…

'That's all great, Bianca, I mean congratulations again and I can't wait to get started. I just remembered, I didn't pack for a week-long stay and there's a few things I need, so I'm just going to go out and grab them…' She collected her bag and backed out of the door still babbling inanely. 'When I get back we'll talk lace, okay? I won't be long.' The last thing she saw as the door swung shut behind her was Bianca, upright and staring at her in complete surprise.

Smoothly done, Sophie.

But she couldn't wait, not another second, not while this big *what if* was thundering through her body, beating its question with every thud of her heart.

Although she found her way out of the *palazzo* easily enough, having earmarked enough landmarks to find her way to the main hallway and back up to her room, as soon as she set foot outside it was a different matter. Sophie plunged into the alleyways and back streets searching for the green cross that meant pharmacy in a dozen different languages. But each road seemed to lead her nowhere, a dead end with water rippling gently at the end, round in a gently curving circle back to the same square over and over.

And what would happen when she reached

a pharmacy? She could barely order a pizza in Italian let alone a pregnancy test and she doubted her mime skills were up to scratch.

You're being ridiculous, she told herself. *You used protection, you were careful, he was careful.*

But the rest of Bianca's words came back, almost visible, floating around her in the still, cold air. Emotional? Check, look at the pity party she'd held for herself on New Year's Eve, the tears just now. Light-headed and tired? For a couple of weeks now. Nauseous? Yes, a low level, almost constant feeling of sickness. All kinds of things set it off. She hadn't been able to stomach even the smell of wine for ages; it had been an oddly teetotal Christmas and New Year's Eve.

Sophie stopped dead in the middle of the street. Of course she was pregnant. How could she not have known—and what on earth was she going to do now?

'Sophie, Bianca mentioned you wanted to visit Burano. Would this afternoon be convenient?'

Sophie skidded to a stop outside the salon and fought an urge to hide her handbag behind her back as if Marco might see through the leather, to the paper bag within. It had been a mortifying experience, but thanks to the Internet, her phone, some overly helpful shoppers and a very patient pharmacist she had finally got what she needed.

Well, two of what she needed. She hadn't paid that much attention in Science, but she was pretty sure all experiments could go wrong.

'Marco! Hi! Yes, Burano, this afternoon, sounds wonderful, great.'

One eyebrow rose. 'Are you okay?' He sauntered over to the salon door and she had to fight the urge to step away.

'Fine, I've been out. I got a little lost, that's all.'

'The best way to learn Venice is to get lost in her,' he said, but there was a quizzical gleam in his dark eyes as he looked at her.

'In that case we'll soon be the best of friends.' Sophie knew she was acting oddly, but she needed to get out of this hallway and up into the safety of her room and find out for once and for all. 'What time do you want to leave?'

'If we leave here just after noon, we could stop for lunch along the way.'

'That sounds wonderful. I just need to talk to Bianca then, take another look at the dress and get a swatch of material. Shall I meet you back here in an hour? Great. See you then.'

She barely registered his response as she walked as fast as she could up the stairs, slowing a little as she tackled the second and then the third staircase until finally she was twisting open the door to her room, throwing her bag onto the bed, grabbing the paper bag and rushing into the bathroom, tearing open the plastic on the box as she did so…

She was pregnant. Two tests' worth of pregnant.

Sophie sank onto the bed with a strangled sob, throwing her hand across her mouth to try to keep the noise in. Idiot. Fool. Stupid, stupid girl. It was different for Bianca. She was engaged to a man she loved, she had a great career, a life ready and waiting for a baby. What did Sophie have? A fling with a commitment-shy man she barely knew, a shoebox of a flat, an unfulfilled dream and a job scrubbing toilets and serving drinks. How was she going to fit a baby into her flat, let alone her life?

She slumped down on the bed and stared up at the ceiling, every fat cherub leg, every beaming cherub grin on the fresco an unneeded reminder. The thing was she *did* want children. Had planned to have them with Harry—although she had never got him to admit the time was right. Thank goodness. She shuddered; if she had had his baby, would she ever have got out? Ever freed herself or would she still be there now? Holding down a job, taking care of the house, looking after the kids while Harry lied and cheated and manipulated...

But Marco wasn't like Harry. He was, well, he was... 'Face it,' Sophie said aloud. 'You know nothing about him except he doesn't want to get married. He's rich. He's handsome. He's good in bed. He seems kind, when it suits him to be...' Added together it didn't seem an awful lot to know about the father of her baby.

Father. Baby. She swallowed a hysterical sob.

She had to tell him; it was the right, the fair, thing to do.

And then what? He might walk away although, she conceded, he didn't seem the type. Sophie wrapped her arms around herself, trying to hug some warmth into her suddenly chilled body. He might accuse her of entrapment. Think this was done on purpose…

He didn't want to get married, she knew that, and that was okay. After all, they didn't really know each other. But what about when his mother found out? She wanted grandchildren, heirs, and here Sophie was carrying a Santoro heir as a good little wife should.

She shivered again, nausea rolling in her stomach. She'd been free for one year and six months, independent for such a short while. No placating, no begging, no reassuring, no abasing, no making herself less so someone else could be more. No eggshells. She was pretty sure Marco wasn't another Harry, she knew his mother had all the best intentions, but if they knew she was pregnant, she would have every choice stripped away, be suffocated with kindness and concern and responsibility until every bit of that hard-won independence shrivelled away and she belonged to them. Just as she had belonged to Harry. Besides, Bianca was getting married in a week. This was her time. It wouldn't be fair to spoil her wedding with the inevitable drama Sophie's news would cause.

I won't tell him yet, she decided. *I need to know him first, know who the real Marco is. Know if I can trust him. I'll get to know him over this week and then I'll tell him. After the wedding.*

Marco manoeuvred his boat out of the Grand Canal with practised ease. It came more naturally than driving, even after a decade in London. Sometimes he thought he felt truly alive only when he was here on the water, the sun dancing on the waves around him, Venice at his back, the open lagoon his for the taking.

'Warm enough?' He'd elected not to take the traditional, bigger family boat with its polished wood and spacious covered seating area. Instead they were in his own small but speedy white runabout, which didn't have any shelter beyond the splash screen at the front. He'd reminded Sophie to wrap up warmly for the journey over, but she was so pale and silent maybe she'd underestimated the bite of the January wind out in the lagoon.

'Hmm? No, thanks, honestly I'm toasty.' He could see her visibly push away whatever was occupying her thoughts as she turned to him and smiled. 'Bianca says Burano is beautiful. I'm really looking forward to seeing it.'

'It is,' he assured her. 'Very different from Venice, but equally stunning in a quieter way.'

'Did you visit the islands a lot when you were younger? What about the rest of Italy? It's such a beautiful country. It must have been wonderful to have had it all on your doorstep,' she added quickly as he raised an eyebrow at her series of questions.

'It is beautiful and, yes, most of our childhood holidays were spent in Italy. Venice gets so hot and busy in the summer and we have a villa by Lake Como, so every summer we would spend a month there. And I don't remember a time when

I didn't explore the islands. Every Venice child grows up able to handle a boat before they learn to ride a bike.'

'And swim?'

'*Sì*, and swim.'

'I still can't imagine what it was like, actually living here, crossing water to get to school. It just seems impossibly exotic.'

'Not when it's your normal. To me, your childhood in Manchester would have seemed equally exotic. What was your route to school? A bus?'

'I doubt it. Suburbia is suburbia, nothing exciting there. But a school boat? Now, that's fun.' And once again she turned his question aside effortlessly. Was there some dark secret there or did she really think her past was of so little interest? 'What else did you do when you were little? Were you a football player or addicted to video games or a bookworm?'

'None of the above. If I wasn't messing around on a boat, I was always trying to find a way to do some kind of deal.' He grinned at her surprised expression. 'I told you, we're an island of merchants, sailors, traders. Oh, it's been several hundred years since we had any influence, since we controlled the waves, but it's still there in any true Venetian's veins.'

'What did your parents say?'

'Oh, they were proud,' he assured her. 'So many families forgot their roots, watched the *palazzos* crumble around them as the money ran out. My mother is a big believer in a good day's work, no matter who you are.' Proud right until she realised his independent entrepreneurial streak wasn't just a phase.

It was as if Sophie had read his mind. 'Was she disappointed when you set up for yourself? Left Venice?' She leaned against the windscreen, half turned to face him, eyes intent on him as if the answers really mattered.

'Yes. She's convinced one day I'll get over my little rebellion and come home, settle down and take over the family affairs.' He paused as he navigated the boat around a buoy. 'Of course, since my father died she's been keener than ever and at some point I need to make a decision about where my future lies. But right now she's not ready to give up the reins no matter what she says—she'll spend every second of her retirement second-guessing every decision I make. I have a while yet. Besides…' Marco had always known the day would come when he would have to step in, but he wanted to see how big his own business could grow first. He already turned over several million euros annually, and there was plenty of room to expand, new territories to trade in.

'Besides what?'

'Bianca. Maybe she could take over the Santoro holdings. She's an extremely talented businesswoman, she's got exactly the same heritage as me and I know she wants a family, so she could hand the business on, just as my parents wanted.'

'That makes sense. Hasn't your mother ever considered it?'

'Neither of my parents have. In many ways they were very old-fashioned. Bianca's a woman, so in their eyes when she marries she'll no longer be a true Santoro. But it's just a name…' And if Bianca did take over the business, the *palazzo* and provide the heirs, then he would be free.

Was it the perfect solution—or was he merely fulfilling his father's prophecies and eluding his responsibilities? Marco had no idea. It all seemed so clear, so simple in London, but the second he set foot back in Venice he got tangled up in all the threads of loyalty, duty and family he'd spent most of his life struggling to free himself from.

They had reached the open waters of the lagoon and Marco let out the throttle, allowing the boat to zoom ahead. 'I miss this,' he admitted. 'This freedom.'

'I can imagine. I know there's a harbour in Chelsea, but sailing up and down the Thames must be a little sedate after living here. What do you like to do in London for fun? Apart from attending parties, that is.'

Marco eased off on the throttle and let the boat slow as Burano came into view. 'Is this an interview?' He was teasing but noted the high colour that rose over her cheeks with interest. 'An interrogation? Will you lock me up in the Doge's palace if I answer wrongly?'

'Yes, right next to Casanova. No, no interrogation, I'm just interested. We're spending all this time together and I know nothing about you. I need to be prepared if you want your mother to think we're a real couple. What if she gets me alone? Imagine how suspicious she would be if I don't know your favourite football team, or how you take your coffee.'

'Black, strong, no sugar and of course I support Venezia despite our current ranking. Thank goodness our national team is a little more inspiring.' Sophie was right, he realised. If they were acting the couple, it made sense to know more about each other. Besides, she was fun company, insightful with a dry wit he appreciated. 'How about you? City or United?'

'Me?' She blinked. 'My family is City, so I am by default, but to be honest I'm not really bothered. We were a bit divided on gender lines when I was a child. My father would take my brothers to matches, but I was eight years younger and so I was always left behind with my mother, who was definitely *not* interested. I think she thought sport was invented to ruin her weekends.'

'Did that annoy you? Being left out by your brothers?'

She wrinkled her nose. 'No one likes being the baby of the family, do they? But my mother encouraged it, I think. By the time I was born my brothers' lives revolved around sport. Footie, cricket, rugby—it's all they talked about, watched, did. She always said she was delighted to have a daughter, an ally at last.' She sounded wistful, her eyes fixed on the sea.

'You weren't into sport, then?'

Sophie shrugged. 'I didn't really have the option. Like I said, Dad would take the boys to matches or whatever and Mum and I would be left behind. Besides, she was determined not to lose me to their side. She had me in classes of her choosing as soon as I could walk. Dance,' she confirmed at his enquiring look. 'I wasn't kidding when I told you at the Snowflake Ball that I'd done every kind of dancing.'

'A dancer? Professionally?' It made sense. She had the build, petite as she was, strong and lithe, and he dimly remembered her mentioning it on New Year's Eve.

'Could have been. Mum thought I'd be a ballerina. She wanted me to train properly at sixteen, dance at Covent Garden one day.'

'But you didn't want to?'

She shook her head. 'It's not just about talent, it's luck, build, you know, having the right body, discipline but most of all drive. I was good, but good enough? Probably not. I didn't want it enough. I stopped just before I turned sixteen. It broke her heart.'

She looked down at her hands and he didn't pursue it—he knew all about breaking parental hearts, was a gold medallist in it. 'What did you want to do instead?' It wasn't just about polite conversation; he was actually interested. His hands tightened on the wheel as the realisation dawned.

Sophie smiled, slow and nostalgic. 'The thing I did really like about ballet, about performing, was the costumes. Every show involves a lot of net and tulle and gluing sequins—I loved that part. I was always much happier with a needle than a pointe shoe. So I guess I'm lucky, trying to make a go of the thing I love. If I'd become a ballet dancer, I'd be over halfway through my career by now. Not that I can imagine I'd have had much of one. Like I say, I was never driven enough.' She stopped and stared as they neared the pretty harbour and the brightly coloured fishermen's cottages came into view. 'Oh, my goodness, how beautiful. Where's my camera?' She turned away, grabbing her camera and exclaiming over the colours, the boats, the sea, the sky.

As he guided the boat into the harbour, mooring it at a convenient stop, Marco's thoughts were preoccupied with Sophie, still chattering excitedly and snapping away. Why was he so intrigued by her? Sure, she was fun, they had chemistry and she was proving extremely helpful in calming Bianca's ever more volatile nerves and keeping his mother off his back. But next week she would return to London and their brief relationship would be over. There was no point in prolonging it when they both knew they weren't heading anywhere. Short, sweet and to the point just as all perfect liaisons should be.

But what would it be like not to feel as if every relationship was ticking towards an expiration date, not to worry about getting in too deep, about not raising expectations he had no intention of fulfilling? For every new woman to be an adventure, a world to be explored, not a potential trap? He'd never cared before, happy with the limits he set upon himself, upon his time, upon his heart. But, for the first time in a really long time, as he helped Sophie ashore, felt the warm clasp of her hand, watched her face alight with sheer happiness as she took in every detail on the colourful island, Marco was aware that maybe, just maybe, he was missing some colour in his perfectly organised, privileged, grey life.

CHAPTER EIGHT

IT WAS THE MOST beautiful commute in the world. How many people travelled to their office by boat? Marco took a deep breath, his lungs glad of the fresh salty air, a much-needed contrast to the polluted London air he usually breathed in on his way to work. No, he thought as he steered his boat across the lagoon towards the dock at the mainland Venetian district of Mestre, this was a much better way to spend his early mornings.

Marco hadn't intended to work from the Santoro Azienda offices, but he found it easier to concentrate away from the *palazzo*. Bianca was staying at home until her wedding and every room was full of tulle or confetti or wedding favours—it was like living in a five-year-old girl's dream doll's house. Besides, working at the *palazzo* meant working in close proximity to Sophie and that, he was discovering, was distracting. And if his mother and sister were at home, then they kept interrupting him to ask his opinion on everything from how the napkins should be folded to where Gia Ana should be seated, given that she had fallen out with every other member of the family.

And when they *weren't* at home, then it was almost impossible for him not to seek Sophie out on some barely disguised pretext—or for her to casually wander by him—knowing that within seconds their eyes would meet, hold, and, like teenagers taking advantage of an empty house, they would drag each other into the nearest bedroom… There was something particularly thrilling about the illicitness of it all, the sneaking down corridors, the stolen kisses, the hurried pulling off clothes or pulling them back on again. Not that his mother or Bianca were fooled for a moment, but that wasn't the point. It was all about appearances. His mother would only countenance an engaged couple sleeping together under her roof. Or not sleeping…

Yes, working at the *palazzo* certainly had its

benefits, but he had far too much to do to allow himself to be continuously distracted, so, for the last couple of days, knowing his mother was so busy with the final details for the wedding she was unlikely to be at work, he had taken to heading off to the office early, returning home during the long lunch break to meet up with Sophie, who was spending most of her mornings working on Bianca's dress. He didn't have to come home, she'd assured him, she was happy to explore Venice on her own if he was too busy, but he was enjoying rediscovering his city, seeing it through her eyes as she absorbed the sights and smells of the city.

The Santoro Azienda offices were a short walk away from the dock. As his parents' real estate and other business interests had expanded and they had taken on more and more staff it had become increasingly clear they needed professional offices out of the *palazzo*. The decision to base the offices on the mainland hadn't been taken lightly, but for the sake of their staff, many of whom no longer lived on the islands, it had made sense and twenty years ago they had moved into the light, modern, purpose-built building. All glass and chrome, it was as different from the *palazzo* as a building could be.

Until last week Marco hadn't set foot in the offices in ten years. It was one of the many things he'd regretted since he'd shouldered his father's coffin to walk it down the aisle towards the altar—and yet he still couldn't see any other way, how he could have played things differently. It took two to compromise and he hadn't been the only one at fault.

Marco strode through the sliding glass doors and, with a nod at the security guard and the receptionists, headed straight for the lifts and the top floor, exiting into the plush corridors that marked the Santoro Azienda's Executive Floor. Left led to his parents' offices, right to the suite of rooms he was using. He hadn't turned left once since he'd returned to the building.

He stood and hesitated, then, with a muffled curse, turned left.

His parents had had adjoining offices on opposite corners of the building, sharing a PA, a bathroom and a small kitchen and seating area. He'd been in his teens when they'd relocated here, spending many days in one office or the other being put to work, being trained up to manage the huge portfolio of properties and companies they owned. No one had ever asked him if it was what he wanted. If they had noticed that he was happier rolling his sleeves up and engaging on the ground level, they ignored it. He was destined to take over and his interest in art and antiques, in dealing directly with people, was a quirk, a hobby.

'A multimillion-euro hobby, Papà,' he said softly. Not that it would have made any difference.

His father's name was still on his office door and Marco stood there for a long moment staring at the letters before twisting the handle and, with a deep breath, entering the room. It was a shock to see that nothing had changed, as if his father could walk in any moment, espresso in hand. The desk still heaped with papers, the carafe of water filled on the oak sideboard, the comfy chair by the window, where his father had liked to sit after lunch and face the city while he took his siesta. Photographs covered the walls, views of Venice, of buildings they owned, goods they made, food prepared in restaurants they owned. There were no photographs of Marco or Bianca. 'The office is for work,' his father used to say. And work he had, in early, out late, deals and successes and annoyances his favourite topic of conversation over the evening meal.

Marco picked up a piece of paper and stared at it, not taking in the typed words. Was his mother coping, doing the work of two people? She hated delegating as much as his father had, didn't like handing too much power to people not part of their family.

They were as stubborn as each other.

He barely registered her footsteps, but he knew she was there before she spoke.

'Marco.'

He closed his eyes briefly. 'Hello, Mamma.'

He turned, forced a smile. In the bright artificial office light he could see the lines on her forehead, the hollows in her cheeks. She was working too hard, still grieving for his father.

'You've been home for two weeks and yet I

barely see you.' Her voice might be full of re-proach, but her eyes were shrewd, assessing his every expression.

'I've been busy. As have you.'

'*Sì*, weddings don't organise themselves. Maybe you'll find that out one day.' She linked her arm through his and gave a small tug. 'Come, Marco, take coffee with me. Let's have a proper catch-up.'

Words guaranteed to strike a chill through any dutiful child's heart. 'No coffee for me, Mamma. I have a lot to do.'

She stepped back and looked up at him. It was many years since she had topped him yet he still had the urge to look up—she carried herself as if she were seven feet tall. 'You work too hard, Marco. A young man like you should be out, enjoying himself. Sophie must be feeling sadly neglected.'

'I doubt it. She's making herself a dress for Bianca's wedding. I'm not sure I would be of much help.'

'Clever girl. She's so creative.' Her eyes flick-ered over his face and Marco stayed as expressionless as possible. 'We lack that in our family. We're all good at facts, at figures, at making money, but none of us has any creativity. It would be nice...' Her voice trailed off, but he knew exactly what she meant. Nice to breed that creativity in. 'She has such lovely colouring as well, the peaches-and-cream English complexion.' As if Sophie were a brood mare, waiting to be mated with a prize stallion.

The old feelings of being imprisoned, stifled, descended like physical bars, enclosing him in, trying to strip all choice away. His mouth narrowed as he fought to keep his cool. 'Yes, she's very pretty.'

'Oh, Marco, she's beautiful. And so sweet. Bianca adores her, says she is just like a sister. We'll all miss her when she returns to London. We'll miss you as well. It's been lovely having you home.'

'Luckily for Bianca they have invented these marvellous little devices which make it possible to communicate over large distances. In fact she usually has one glued to her hand. I'm sure she can speak to Sophie as much as she would like to.'

His mother walked over to the desk and picked up the fountain pen his father had always used. 'My own mother always said one of her greatest joys was watching you and Bianca grow up.'

This was a new one. 'Nonna was a very special person. I miss her.'

'She was in her early twenties when I was born, and I, of course, was very young when I had you. She was still only in her forties when she became a grandmother. Young enough to be active, to be able to play with you. Of course, her dearest wish was to see you marry, have a family of your own.'

'She was taken from us too early.'

'I will be sixty next year, Marco. Sixty.'

He was impressed; she didn't usually admit to her age. 'And you don't look a day over forty-five. Are you sure you have the right year?'

But she wasn't in the mood for gallantry, barely raising a smile at the compliment. 'I want to see my grandchildren, Marco. I want to know them, watch them grow up, not be an old lady, too tired and ill to be able to play when they finally arrive.'

Marco sighed. 'Mamma…'

'I want you back home, back here, where you belong, heading up the Santoro family. I want you settled down and married with children of your own.'

'I know you do. It's all you've ever wanted.'

'I just want you to be happy, Marco.'

He fought to keep his voice even. 'I know. But you have to accept that happiness comes in many different forms, in many different ways. I like what I do. I like London.'

'And what of me? Of the business?'

'There are other options. Bianca, for instance. Come on, Mamma, you must have considered it. Bianca is more than fit to take over from you. She's the best of us all when it comes to figures, she's ambitious and she's a Santoro to her fingernails, no matter who she marries and what her last name is. Don't overlook her. You'll be doing all of us a disservice.'

His mother only smiled. 'You think I haven't considered her? That your father didn't? Of course we have. You're right, in many ways she's the cleverest of us all and when it comes to the finances there's no one I would rather have in charge. But she doesn't have what your father had—what you have—she doesn't have the flair, the inspired spark.'

Guilt flared as she compared him to his father and Marco's hands curled into fists involuntarily. 'I don't know what you mean.'

'Yes, you do,' she said, staring at him as if she could imprint her words into him. 'Bianca and I can manage, we can audit, we can run—but you and your father can build. Can take an idea and make it grow, see where opportunity lies and grab it with both hands. I'm not discounting Bianca because she's a woman and getting married, I'm discounting her because she won't grow the company like you will. Because you are the heir your father wanted.'

Bitterness coated his mouth. 'Papà didn't want me to be inspired. He didn't want me to be anything but an obedient clone. He sat in this room, at this desk, and told me if I went to England, continued to mess around with antiques, we were finished.'

'They were just words. You know what he was like. Words came too easily and he never meant them—it was what he did which counted. And he was proud of you, Marco. He followed your every move. People would tell him of you, people you worked with in Venice, further afield, would seek him out to talk of you and he would drink in every word.'

The ache in Marco's chest eased, just a little. 'He never said, never showed that he even knew what I was doing…'

'You didn't give him the opportunity. Besides…' she shrugged '…he was too proud to make the first move. He was proud, you are proud and here you are.'

'He sat there and disowned me and when I disobeyed him he…' But he couldn't say the words.

'He had a heart attack,' she finished calmly. 'It wasn't your fault, Marco.'

Easy for her to say. He knew better; he'd always known. 'Of course it was. If I had settled to be what he wanted…'

'Then you wouldn't be you. He knew that. But it hurt him that you barely returned. That from the moment you went to London you never again spent a night under our roof.'

Misunderstandings, pride, stubbornness. Family traits passed on from father to son. 'I couldn't. I didn't dare. I couldn't let his health blackmail me into compliance, nor could I let him work himself into one of his passions. It was better to stay away.' He stopped, bleak. 'He died anyway.'

'*Sì*. But not because of anything you said or didn't say but because he didn't listen to his doctor, didn't listen to me, didn't exercise or take his pills or cut down on red meat. Stubborn. But it's not your fault, Marco. That first heart attack would have happened anyway, you must know that. We're lucky we had him for another ten years.'

But Marco hadn't had him; he'd lost his father long before. 'And now it's too late, he's gone and he didn't even know I said goodbye.'

Her eyes were soft with understanding, with love. 'He knew. You came straight away. He was conscious enough to know you were there. Forgive yourself, Marco. Nobody else blames you for any of it, nobody ever did. But I would like you to come home, at least to be here more often. To advise me even if you won't take over. I just want to see my son more than a couple of hours once or twice a year.'

'Yes.' His mind was whirling. Why had his father never told him that he was proud of him, never said he hadn't meant a word of the bitter denunciation that had left him in the hospital and Marco in exile? But his mother was right. Marco hadn't stayed away just out of fear he would trigger another heart attack, he'd stayed away out of pride. Just as bad as his father. Maybe it was time to let some of that pride go.

'Yes,' he said again. 'I can be here more often. And I can't promise you I'll take over, but I can advise—and make sure you have the right people in place to help you. You need to delegate more, Mamma, and accept that people who aren't Santoros can still care about the company.'

'It's a deal.'

Relief flooded through him. They had compromised and, for the first time, he didn't feel that she had tried to manipulate him; she had respected his decision. He would, should spend more time in Venice. It was only right that he at least took a board role in his family company.

He bent, kissed his mother's cheek and turned to leave but stopped as she called his name softly. 'Marco?'

'Yes?'

'Ten years wasted, Marco, out of pride, out of anger...' She paused. 'Don't make that mistake again. I know you say you aren't ready to marry and I know you are angry with me, with your father, for what happened ten years ago. But don't let that pride, that anger, push Sophie away. She's a lovely girl, Marco. But I don't think there will be second chances with that one. You need to get it right.'

'Mamma, we've only just met.'

'I know, and I am staying out of it.' Despite his prickle of annoyance he couldn't help an incredulous laugh at her words. 'Just think about it. That's all I'm asking. Just take care with her.'

'Okay.' He could promise that with an easy mind. Taking care came easily to him; he knew how to tread for an easy relationship and an easier exit. 'I'll take care. Now I really have to get on.' But as he walked away her words echoed in his mind. *No more second chances.* He didn't need a second chance. He liked Sophie, he liked her a lot, enough to know that she deserved a lot better than anything a man like him could offer. He should thank her though, for all her help. He might not be able to offer her happy ever after—and she probably wouldn't take it if he did—but he could offer her one perfect day. It was the least he could do. It had to be; it was all that he had.

CHAPTER NINE

TO SOPHIE'S AMAZEMENT Marco was still in the breakfast room when she came down, having overslept again. She stopped and hovered at the door, stupidly shy.

How she could feel shy when he'd left her bedroom just four short hours ago, how she could still feel shy after the things they'd done in that bedroom, eluded her and yet her stomach swooped at the sight of him and her tongue was suddenly too large for her mouth, like a teenager seeing her crush across the hallway.

They hadn't eaten breakfast together since that first morning. He was usually already out working when she came downstairs, their first communication of the day at lunch. Lunch was civilised, easy to navigate, but breakfast? Breakfast was an intimate meal. She wasn't ready for breakfast…

His presence wasn't the only thing that had changed. The atmosphere in the *palazzo* seemed lighter somehow, less fraught. Less weighted with the air of things left unsaid, when the silences were more eloquent than words. For the first time since the party she and Marco had stayed at the *palazzo* for dinner last night and Marco hadn't tensed up too much when his mother had quizzed Sophie once more about her future plans and shot him meaningful glances every time she did so. Marco's mother was very charming, but over the space of the evening she'd ramped up the inquisitional levels to almost overbearing, her hints so broad Sophie hadn't known where to look half the time. She'd aimed for obliviousness, but it was difficult to look unknowing when she was invited to try on Marco's dead grandmother's engagement ring, asked about her perfect honeymoon plans or how many children she wanted and didn't she think her eyes with Marco's colouring would look cute in a baby?

She might, possibly, have been able to laugh the whole thing off if it weren't for the pregnancy. Guilt, embarrassment and fear mingled in a toxic concoction every time Marco's mother opened her mouth. Every time Signora Santoro mentioned children guilt shot through Sophie, like a physical pain. It took everything she had to sit and pretend everything was okay, not to jump up and announce her pregnancy in a rush of tears. She still thought it was fair to wait until after the wedding, it was just a week's delay after all, but she knew in her heart she was deceiving Marco, lying to him by omission.

And part of her knew it wasn't Bianca's welfare really driving her, it was fear. She'd spent so long living her mother's dreams, only to crush them when she'd walked away, the rift still no way near repaired. Then she'd allowed Harry to set her course, making him the sole focus of her life. This family was so certain, so overbearing, so grand and overwhelming—what if they tried to take control as soon as they knew about the baby? Had the last year and a half given her enough strength to hold firm and make her own choices?

Time would tell, but she needed these days to

prepare. To try to work out exactly what she, Sophie Bradshaw, wanted, before the Santoro expectations descended onto her.

She took a deep breath and walked into the room, hooking a chair and sitting down, swiping a piece of brioche off Marco's plate as she did so. The key to fighting off both the tiredness and nausea, she'd realised, was carbs and plenty of them. The way she was eating she'd be sporting plenty of bumps long before the baby actually started to show.

'Good morning. All on your own?'

Marco folded his newspaper up and pushed it to one side. Sophie really liked the way he focussed his full attention on the people he was with, apologising if he checked his phone or took a call. He never kept his phone on the table when they were out, never scrolled through it when she was speaking. Harry had never made any secret of the fact every contact in his phone, every game, every meme, every football result came before her. 'You just missed Mamma and Bianca. They told me to remind you that you can join them at any time. Apparently the twenty times they asked you last night wasn't a pressing enough invitation. Are you sure you don't want to go with them?'

Sophie grinned. 'Your mother, Bianca's future mother-in-law, all five of her future sisters-in-law and her three best friends all alternately talking in Italian so I sit there gaping like a goldfish before switching to English to quiz me on your intentions and my potential wedding plans? There's not a spa luxurious enough to tempt me.' She realised how ungrateful that sounded and backtracked quickly. 'I like them all well enough, in fact I love Bianca and your mother individually...'

'But together they strike fear into the heart of the bravest warrior?'

'They really do. Besides, the day after tomorrow it's the wedding and I fly back to London the morning after that. I'm making final adjustments to Bianca's and the bridesmaids' dresses tomorrow, which makes this my last free day here. I want to make the most of it. Explore Venice one final time.'

'Do you want some company?'

Happiness fizzed up at the casual words. 'Of course, but don't you need to work? Don't worry about me if so…'

Giuliana, one of the maids, set a cup, a small teapot and a plate laden with sweet bread, slices of fruit, cheese and a couple of pastries in front of Sophie. Her preference for herbal tea first thing had caused some consternation in the caffeinated household at first, but the staff had eventually adjusted to both tea and her very un-Venetian need for a breakfast more substantial than a few bites of something quick. Sophie nodded her thanks, grateful as the familiar ginger aroma wafted up, displacing the bitter scent of coffee and settling her queasy stomach.

'A few days off seems like the perfect plan right now,' Marco said as Sophie started to tuck in. 'I need time to think about where my business is headed, how I can continue to grow and still meet my obligations to the family business.' His mouth twisted into a rueful smile. 'I realised yesterday that even if I don't want to take over I still need to be involved. Besides, when I started out I used my contacts here to source antiques, but it was important for me to be in London to build contacts for the other side of the business, the people I would sell to. I've been based there ten years, own a house in Chelsea. In many ways it's my home.'

Right there and then the chasm between them widened even further. Sophie rented a shoebox on the top floor of a building on a busy road. Buses thundered past at all hours of the day and night, streetlights lit up her room, casting an orange glow over her dreams, and the bass from the flat below provided a thudding soundtrack to everything she did. Half her pay went straight to her landlord. Owning a home of her own was a distant enough dream, her city shoebox well out of her range. A whole house? In Chelsea? Not for the likes of her.

It was all going to make telling him about the baby even harder. If only they were equals financially... She pushed the thought away, adding it to her ever-lengthening list of things to worry about in the future. 'But now?'

'I still need an office and a base in London, but those contacts are secure. I have a whole global network of dealers, buyers, designers who know and trust me. I'm having to work a little harder on the Italian side now. There's a new generation of suppliers coming along and I don't have the same links with them, the same trust. It means I'm no longer the automatic first choice and that could impact my future stock.'

'So, you need to spend more time here?' Her heart twisted. She had no idea what her future held, but she hadn't expected to have a baby with a man she wasn't committed to, a man who spent half his life out of the country.

Suck it up, she told herself fiercely. *This will be your reality. Deal with it.*

'I do. But these are thoughts for another day. I'm very much aware how much we owe you, Sophie. Bianca would have imploded if you hadn't stayed. Let me make it up to you. Anything you want. How do you want to spend the day? A trip to the lakes? To Roma? Buy out the whole of the lace shops on Burano?'

Guilt twisted again. She'd had her own selfish reasons for staying, for getting close to Marco's family. But she couldn't pass up this opportunity to spend a day with the father of her child—and she didn't want to. She wanted to spend the day with him, to get to know him a little better, to have one last carefree day before she shattered his world. 'Nothing so elaborate. Show me your Venice, Marco, the things you love most about the city. That's what I'd like to do today. If you're okay with that.'

'Really? That's what you want to do? You're willing to take the risk?' He looked surprised, but he was smiling. 'In that case I'll meet you back here in half an hour. Wear comfy shoes and wrap up warm. We may be out for some time.'

CHAPTER TEN

SOPHIE INSTANTLY FELL in love with the Dorsoduro. Although there were plenty of tourists around, exclaiming over the views and taking selfies with the canals and bridges as backdrops, it had a more relaxed air than the streets around the Rialto Bridge and Saint Mark's square, a sense of home and belonging, especially once they reached the quieter back streets and small tree-lined squares. Amongst the grocery and souvenir shops, the cafés and restaurants, she spotted some gorgeous boutiques, specialising in stationery, in paints, in textiles as well as enticing pastry and confectionery shops that made her mouth water and she itched to explore further. 'Can I go shopping before lunch and then explore this afternoon? I'd really like to look at those textiles if I could.'

'Of course. I'm not sure how we've managed

to miss this area out of our tours,' Marco said. 'We spent some time in the east of the *sestieri*, but somehow we haven't wandered here.'

'That's because we were meant to come here today. It's been waiting for me all week, an old friend I haven't met yet.'

'That's exactly what this area is, an old friend. If I ever lived back in Venice full-time, I wouldn't want to live in the *palazzo*. I'd prefer a little house tucked away in the back streets here. Something smaller than the London house, overlooking a canal.'

No one Sophie had ever met who lived in London had ever wanted something smaller. Curiosity got the better of her manners. 'How big *is* your house in London?'

Marco shrugged. 'Four bedrooms. It's just a terrace, round the back of the King's Road. Three floors and a basement, courtyard garden.'

Sophie managed to keep walking somehow. *Just* a terrace. *Just* round the back of the King's Road. She often walked those streets, picking out her favourites from the ivy-covered, white and pastel painted houses, knowing that houses like that, lifestyles like that, were as beyond her dreams as living on Mars.

She'd known that Marco's family was rich, knew he had enough money to buy handmade suits and frequent expensive bars, but somehow she hadn't realised that Marco was rich—really rich, not merely well off—in his own right.

It made everything infinitely worse.

It took two to make a baby, she reminded herself. This wasn't her fault. She wasn't trying to trap him, to enrich herself at his expense. But it was what people would think. It might be what he would think and she couldn't blame him. It would all be so much easier if he were a little more normal, if his family hadn't made the idea of fatherhood, marriage and settling down into his worst nightmare. If she thought he'd be happy with her news, not horrified...

Preoccupied, she hadn't noticed where they were walking, barely taking in that Marco had turned out of the narrow road to lead her through an arched gate and onto a rough floor made of wooden slats, leading down to the canal. Wooden, balconied buildings took up two sides of the square, the open canals the other two, and upturned gondolas lined up on the floor in neat rows.

'Marco!' A man dressed in overalls, wiping his hands on a rag, just as if this were a normal garage in a normal town, straightened and strode over, embracing Marco in a warm hug. Marco returned the embrace and the two men began to talk in loud, voluble Italian. Sophie didn't even try to follow the conversation, even when she heard her name mentioned; instead she pulled out her camera and began to take pictures of two young men bending over a gondola, faces intent as they applied varnish to the curved hull. It was the closest she'd got to a gondola in all the time she'd been here; Marco owned his own boat, of course, and had made it clear that gondola rides were only for tourists. She'd not argued but couldn't help feeling a little cheated out of the quintessential Venetian experience.

'*Sì...sì, grazie.*' Marco embraced the man again and Sophie whipped the camera round to capture the moment, his body completely relaxed, his smile open and wide in a way it never was at the *palazzo*. His family were only a small part of his world here. He had his business contacts, yes, family obligations and friends—but also this whole other life. His own friends and interests, left behind when he started a new life in London, and yet still obviously important. This was what he would be returning to when he started to spend more time here. Leaving behind the network of business friends he spent his time with in London for people who really knew him. Sophie swallowed. She could go back to Manchester tomorrow and not meet one person who would make her smile the way Marco was smiling now.

'Ready?' He stepped over an oar and re-joined Sophie.

'For what?'

'I thought you wanted to go shopping and I have a few things I need to buy. *Arrivederci,*' he called over his shoulder as they exited the yard as speedily as they had entered it.

Sophie looked back, wishing they'd had more time for her to take in every detail. 'Is that where gondolas go to die?'

His mouth curved into the rare genuine smile she loved to see, the smile she liked to draw out of him. 'No, it's where they go to get better. Tonio's family have been fixing them for generations. When we were boys he swore it wouldn't be for him, swore that he would travel the world, be his own man...'

'What happened?'

Marco shrugged. 'He travelled the world and realised that all he wanted was to come home and run the yard. Now he's the most respected gondola maker and fixer in all of Venice.'

It didn't take long to reach the shops Sophie had noted when they'd first entered the Dorso-duro and she was immediately torn between a textile shop specialising in hand-woven materials and a traditional mask maker. She hadn't had to dip too far into her carefully hoarded money so far; a few ingredients for the meal she'd cooked Marco, material from a warehouse for her dress and for Bianca's wedding gift, but she wanted to buy presents for her friends if possible.

'I have a few errands to run,' Marco said as she

wavered between the two. 'See you back here in an hour? I know the perfect place for lunch.' And before she could respond he was gone. Sophie checked her watch. She had just under an hour and streets of tempting little shops to explore; there was no time to waste. With a deep breath and a feeling of impending bankruptcy she opted for the mask shop.

It was like stepping into another world, a world of velvet and lace, of secrecy and whispers, seductive and terrifying in equal measure. Sophie turned slowly, marvelling at the artistry in every detail, her eyes drawn to a half-face cat mask, one side gold, the other a green brocade, sequins highlighting the slanted eye slits and the perfect feline nose. She picked it up and held it against her face, immediately transformed into someone—something—dangerous and unknown. She replaced it with a sigh of longing. The gorgeous carnival masks, all made and painted by hand, were definitely beyond her means and having seen the real thing she didn't want to waste her money on the cheaper, mass-produced masks displayed on souvenir stalls throughout the city.

Likewise she soon realised that the colourful fabrics, still produced on traditional wooden looms, would bankrupt her.

Three quarters of an hour later she was done, choosing beautiful handmade paper journals, one for each of her friends. Turning as she exited the shop, she saw Marco sauntering towards her, a secretive, pleased smile on his face. 'Done already?' he asked as he reached her side. 'I usually have to drag Bianca and Mamma out of these shops kicking and screaming.'

'I could just look at the colours and the workmanship for hours,' Sophie admitted. 'I very nearly came home with a cat mask. But options for wearing such a thing in London are sadly limited. Not that I can imagine actually wearing it. It's a work of art.'

'You should see the city at *carnivale*. It's not just the masks, the costumes are out of this world—hats, dominoes, elaborate gowns. You would go crazy for the colours and designs. My mother has five different outfits and six different masks, so each year she changes her look completely.'

'What about you? What do you wear?'

'I go for the simple black domino and a half-mask, but it's many years since I've been here during *carnivale*. The city gets a little fevered. It's easy to get carried away.'

After a light lunch at a pretty café overlooking a narrow back-street canal they explored the rest of the vibrant district, wandering down to the university, visiting churches and museums as they went. The afternoon flew by and it was a surprise when Sophie realised it was late afternoon and their wandering no longer had an aimless quality to it. Marco was walking with intent as they retraced their steps back to the gondola yard they had visited earlier. The gates were closed now, but Marco knocked loudly on the wooden door and almost immediately one large gate swung open. Sophie didn't recognise the owner at first. He'd changed out of his overalls and into the striped top and straw hat of a gondolier, although, in a nod to the season, he had put a smart black jacket over the top.

'This way,' Marco said and steered her towards the jetty. A gondola was moored there, gleaming black in the fading light. Warm velvety throws were placed over the black leather seats, several more were folded on the two stools that provided the only other seating. 'It gets cold,' Marco said briefly as he took her hand and helped her step into the gently rocking boat. 'Welcome aboard, *signorina*.'

The rug was soft and warm as Sophie wriggled into one of the two main seats, placed side by side along the middle of the long narrow boat. Marco picked up another blanket and draped it across her knees and Sophie folded her hands into the fabric, glad of the extra coverings. Her tights and wool jacket were good enough protection against the chill while she was moving and the sun was out, but, sitting still as the evening began to reach dark fingers along the sky, she was suddenly very aware it was winter. Marco set a basket on the small table in the middle of the seating area before gracefully stepping aboard and taking his seat next to hers. It was a narrow space and she could feel the hard length of his thigh next to hers, his body heat as he slipped an arm around her shoulders and shouted something unintelligible to his friend. The next moment the moorings were untied and the boat began to glide away from the dock, moving smoothly down the canal.

Marco leaned forward and, with a flourish, took two champagne glasses and a bottle out of the basket, and set them in front of her, followed by a selection of small fruit and custard tarts, beautifully presented in a lavishly decorated box.

'It's far too early for dinner,' he explained. 'But I thought you might enjoy a picnic. And don't worry, I've remembered your 'no drinking in January' rule. The bottle is actually lightly sparkling grape juice, although it really should be Prosecco.'

Sophie didn't need Prosecco, the unexpected sweetness of the surprise he had so carefully planned more intoxicating than any drink could possibly be. The grape juice wasn't too sweet, the tartness a welcome relief against the flaky pastry and sugared fruit of the delicious tarts. Replete, she snuggled back against Marco's arm and watched Venice go by. She'd spent many hours on the canals, but the city felt closer, more magical from the gondola, as if she were in a dream, part of the city's very fabric.

Marco had obviously planned the route with his friend in advance and the gondola took them into several hidden corners of the city, going through water gates into some of the *palazzos* and even slipping beneath churches into secret passages. Their route took them through the back waters and quieter canals and at times it was as if they were the only people in the city, even their gondolier fading into the background as, with a final burst of orange and pink, the sun finally began to sink into the water and the velvety dusk fell.

'I don't know why you said a gondola was a tourist trap. It is the most romantic thing that has ever happened to me,' Sophie said as the last of the day disappeared, their way now lit by the soft gold of the lamps, their reflections glowing in the murky water.

'More romantic than you knocking me over in the snow?'

She pretended to think about it. 'Almost. Even

more romantic than you chasing me into a cupboard on New Year's Eve.'

'I have fond memories of that cupboard,' he said and she elbowed him.

'Nothing happened in that cupboard, unless you're mixing me up with someone else that night.'

'Oh, no, you are definitely one of a kind,' Marco said softly. 'The first girl who ever ran away from me.'

'I find that hard to believe.' But she didn't. She found it hard to believe that she ever had run away, that she had had the strength of will to walk away that first night and again on New Year's Eve. 'Is that why you asked me here, because I walked away?'

'Ran,' he corrected her. 'One sight of me and you were tearing through that ballroom like an Olympic medallist in heels. And maybe that's why. I was intrigued for sure, wanted to spend more time with you.'

And now? She wanted to ask, but she didn't quite dare. The carefully orchestrated romance of the evening was perfect but could so easily be a farewell gesture. 'You didn't bargain for quite so much time,' she said instead. 'Thank you, Marco, I know you were blindsided by your sister, but thank you for making me feel welcome, for making me feel wanted...'

He leaned over then, pulling her close, his mouth on hers, harder than his usual sweet kisses, more demanding. He kissed her as if they were the only two people in the whole of Venice, as if the world might stop if she didn't acquiesce, fall into it, fall into him. The world fell away, the heat of his mouth, his hands holding her still, holding her close all she knew, all she wanted to know. Her own arms encircled him as she buried one hand in his hair, the other clutching at his shoulder as if she were drowning and he all that stood between her and a watery grave.

It was the first time he'd kissed her for kissing's sake, she realised in some dim part of her mind. That first night they didn't lay a hand on each other until they were in the hotel room, New Year's Eve she had walked away from his touch—but if she hadn't, she knew full well they would have ended up in that same hotel room, the kiss a precursor, a promise of things yet to come. It would have been another hotel, not his house; close as it must have been, that was too intimate for Marco, not her flat, too intimate for her.

Even here in Venice they were curiously separate... Oh, he kissed her cheek in greeting, held her arm to guide her, but there were no gestures of intimacy; no holding hands, no caresses as they passed each other, no cuddles or embraces. No kisses on bridges or boats. Kisses, caresses, embraces—they were saved for under cover of darkness, saved for passion and escape. But there could be no passion or escape here in the middle of a canal, visible to anyone and everyone walking by. This was kissing for kissing's sake. Touching for touching's sake. This was togetherness.

Her heart might burst—or it might break—but all she could do was kiss him back and let all her yearning, her need, her want pour out of her and into him. Savour each second—because if this was it, if this was a farewell gesture, she wanted to remember every single moment, remember what was good before she blew his world apart.

Sophie hadn't expected the evening to continue after the gondola ride, but after they reluctantly disembarked Marco took her to a few of his favourite *bàcaro*, small bars serving wine and *cicchetti*, little tapas-type snacks. In one *bàcaro* Sophie was enchanted by the selection of *francobollo*, teeny little sandwiches filled with a selection of meats or roasted vegetables. 'They're so tiny it's like I'm not eating anything at all,' she explained to a fascinated Marco as she consumed her tenth—or was it eleventh? 'Less than a mouthful doesn't count, everyone knows that.' In another she tried the tastiest meatballs she had ever eaten and a third offered a selection of seafood that rivalled the fanciest of restaurants. One day, she promised herself, she would return when the smell of the different house wines didn't make her wrinkle her nose in disgust and she could sample the excellent coffee without wanting to throw up.

She had no idea how long they spent in the

friendly, noisy bars as early evening turned into evening. Marco seemed to know people everywhere they went and introduced her to all of them until she had completely lost track of who was a school friend, who a college friend and who had got who into the most trouble in their teens. Everyone was very welcoming and made an effort to speak in English, but Sophie was very conscious of their curious glances, a confirmation that Marco seldom, if ever, brought girlfriends back to Venice.

'Okay,' Marco announced as Sophie was wondering if she could possibly manage just one more *francobollo*. 'Time to go.' She glanced up, surprised; she'd assumed that this was the purpose of the evening, that they didn't have anywhere else to go.

'Go?' she echoed.

He nodded, his face solemn but his eyes gleaming with suppressed mischief.

Sophie got to her feet. They couldn't possibly be going out for dinner, not after the almost constant snacking starting with the pastries in the gondola and ending with that last small sandwich, and it was too dark to head back out on the water. She was relieved that she'd dressed smartly that morning, and some bright lipstick and mascara had been enough to make her look bar ready; she just hoped it would work for whatever Marco had planned next. 'Okay, I'm ready. Lead on, MacDuff.'

It didn't take them more than five minutes to reach their mystery destination, a grand-looking *palazzo*, just off St Mark's Square. The main door was ajar, guarded by a broad, suited man, and to Sophie's surprise Marco produced two tickets and handed them over. The man examined them and then with a nod of his head opened the door and bade them enter. They were ushered through a grand hallway, beautifully furnished in the formal Venetian style, up the sweeping staircase and into a grand salon, where around sixty people were milling around, all smartly dressed. In the corner a string quartet were tuning their instruments.

One end of the room was empty, furniture carefully placed in a way that reminded Sophie of a stage set; chairs had been placed in semi-circles facing the empty area. 'Is this a recital?'

'Not quite. Have you been to the opera before?'

'The opera? No, never. Is that what this is? In a house?'

'La Traviata,' Marco confirmed. 'Each act takes place in a different room in the *palazzo* so that the audience is both spectator and part of the scene. It's one of my favourite things to do when I'm home. I thought you might enjoy it.'

'Oh, I'm sure I will.' Sophie knew nothing about opera, had no idea if she would like the music, but it didn't matter—what mattered was the effort Marco had put into her last free evening here. The effort he had put in to show her the parts of Venice that meant something to him, show her the city he loved and missed. 'Thank you, Marco. This is the loveliest thing anyone has ever, ever done for me.'

He smiled, but before he could reply they were asked to take their seats.

The next couple of hours passed by in a blur of music, of song, of spectacle, of tears. Sophie was so engrossed she didn't notice the tears rolling down her face as Violetta sang her swansong, not until Marco pressed a handkerchief into her trembling hand. It wasn't just the music, moving as it was, it was the setting, it was the night as a whole, it was the realisation that these were the last innocent hours she and Marco would spend together, that whatever happened after this would be heavy with expectation. She wanted to freeze every second, frame them, remember it all.

'Did you enjoy that?'

She nodded, wrapping her scarf a little tighter as they exited the *palazzo* and turned into St Mark's Square. The moon was low and round, casting an enchantment on the ancient buildings, lit up and golden by the streetlights. 'I loved every bit of it,' she said. 'The whole evening, Marco. Thank you.'

He caught her hand, a boyish carefree gesture, and as he did so realisation rocketed through her, sudden and painful in its clarity. She was in love with him. Deeply, relentlessly, irrevocably in love with him. How had this happened?

Maybe it was hormones, her version of mood swings, an emotion that would drain away when she hit the magic twelve-week mark. Maybe it was fear, fear of raising the baby alone in a tiny flat on a busy main road. Maybe it was simply the novelty of being treated as if she mattered, as if she was worth something by a man worth everything.

Or maybe it was real, that elusive alchemy of desire and compatibility and friendship.

She rose onto her tiptoes, pressing a soft kiss to his bristled cheek in thanks. He moved as she did so, catching her in his arms, capturing her mouth under his so that her light embrace was turned into something more powerful. She allowed him to take control, leaning into him, into his warmth and strength. Allowed him to claim her as his. Because she was, his. But that was almost irrelevant. How could she tell him when he was already burdened by his family's heavy expectations? How could she tell him she loved him when she still had to tell him about the baby? Her love would be one more load for him to bear, one more expectation for him to manage and she couldn't do it to him. She had this night, this kiss. They had to be enough.

CHAPTER ELEVEN

BIANCA QUIVERED AS the music struck up and she clutched his arm even more tightly.

'Hold on in there,' Marco said. 'Not long to go.'

'I'm not nervous, I'm excited. I love Antonio and I can't wait to marry him, to start our life together, I just...' She faltered, her dark eyes tearing up, and he squeezed her hand.

'I know, you wish Papà was here. I do too.'

'He liked Antonio. I'm glad about that. Glad he got to know him, that they respected each other. He'd have liked Sophie too.'

'Bianca, Sophie and I aren't...'

She turned and looked straight at him, beautiful, glowing with her hair caught up behind the heirloom tiara, her veil arranged in foamy folds down her back. 'Not yet, but you could be. I see the way you look at her when you think nobody's watching you.'

'And how's that?'

'You look the way I feel about Antonio, that's how.'

'I think you're seeing what you want to see. I like her, of course I do, I admire her...'

'Fancy the pants off her?' Bianca's mouth curved into a wide grin and she waggled her perfectly plucked eyebrows at him.

'The mouth on you. And a bride at that! Yes, I find her attractive too, but that's not...' He stopped, unable to find the right words.

'That's not what? What falling in love is? I never had you down as the stars and flowers type, Marco. Falling in love might be instantaneous, strike-me-down, can't-live-without-this person, all-consuming lust when you are sixteen, when you're twenty. It's meant to be like that when you're young. But when you grow up, when you're an adult, then love is something slower but stronger. You start off with like and admire and attract and over time it grows and becomes all the more powerful for that. But you have to let it grow, not run away the first chance you get.'

Marco stared down into his little sister's face. 'When did you get so wise?'

She smirked. 'I always was. Now stand up straight and get ready to support me down this aisle. These heels are ridiculous and I have no intention of tripping and prostrating myself at Antonio's feet!'

The music swelled, their cue. He bent slightly and kissed Bianca's cheek. 'Ready, *sorellina*?'

She inhaled slowly, her hand shaking as she did so. 'Ready. Let's go get me married.'

Bianca had chosen to marry in the gorgeous Church of Santa Maria dei Miracoli, partly because of the sumptuous décor and partly, Marco suspected, because she'd liked the idea of standing at the top of the marble staircase to make her vows. There weren't quite enough seats for all the guests and people were standing at the back and along the sides, all three hundred pairs of eyes staring right at Marco and Bianca. Marco barely noticed them; he was searching for the one person he wanted to see, Bianca's words hammering through his brain with every step they took.

Like, admire, attract.

Was she right? Was it that simple? If so, why did the very thought of it feel so terrifying? So insurmountable? And yet…he inhaled, his heart hammering fast, louder than the organ music filling the great church. And yet in some ways it made perfect sense.

As they neared the front of the church he caught sight of Sophie, elegant and poised, standing next to his mother. If he hadn't known that she had whipped her dress up in just two days, he would never have believed it; she looked as if she were wearing the most exclusive designer fashion. She'd opted for a silvery grey damask material, which shimmered faintly under the chandelier lights. It was a seemingly conservative design, wide straps at her neck with the neckline cut high, almost to her throat—a stark contrast to the deep vee at her back, exposing creamy skin down to the midpoint of her spine. The bodice fitted tightly right to her waist and then the material flared out into a full knee-length skirt. The look was deceptively demure—but the dress fitted the contours of her body perfectly, the material lovingly caressing every slight curve. She'd twisted her hair up into a loose chignon confined by a silver band showing off the graceful lines of her neck. She was elegant and sophisticated, easily outshining the more elaborate and colourful dresses crowding the pews of the ornate church.

She looked right at him and smiled, a soft intimate smile, and his chest tightened. Two days ago he had promised her a perfect day. It hadn't been altogether altruistic; payment for all the work she had put in on the wedding, work that had ended up going way beyond altering one dress; distraction for him as he mulled over the momentous decision to step back into the family business, to spend more time at home; seduction, he'd wanted the kind of day that would make her boneless with desire because sex with her was out of this world and they had so little time left. No, his reasons hadn't been altogether altruistic.

But she hadn't demanded fine wines and five-star restaurants, she'd asked him to show her his world. He hadn't realised it at the time, but the price of her day was far higher than the most expensive restaurant in Italy. He'd paid her in intimacy, in revealing parts of his soul he kept hidden from the whole world.

Like, admire, attract.

Surely, despite the short amount of time he'd known her they had gone way beyond those three words and he'd no idea how it had happened, how he'd let his guard down. He'd kept himself so safe, most of the women he'd met over the last decade or so had as little interest in his inner life as he had in theirs. They cared about his name, his family, his prospects, his money. They made superficiality all too easy, all too attractive.

But Sophie wasn't like that. She was visibly shocked by his wealth, unimpressed by his name. And still he hid. Because if she found him wanting, it would matter; this time it could hurt.

Marco escorted Bianca up the stairs towards the altar and her waiting groom. She'd forgotten about him, about the church full of people waiting to see her get married, all her attention on Antonio, her eyes shining and luminous. He crossed himself as they neared the altar and, as if in a dream, waited to play his small part, before descending the steps to join Sophie and his mother, leaving Bianca making her vows, readying herself for a life in the family she chose, not the one she was born to.

The church hushed, the only sound the voices of the priest, Bianca and her new husband as they repeated vows with heartbreaking sincerity and emotion. All his sister's usual theatrics had disappeared as she gazed at the man she was promising to love in sickness and in health.

'I couldn't understand a word, but that was beautiful.' Sophie gulped as the crowd burst into enthusiastic applause as Bianca and Antonio embraced for the first time as husband and wife. 'She looks so gorgeous. Like the perfect bride. And they look so happy…' Her voice wavered. Next to her one of Marco's aunts was sobbing, on his other side his mother was still applying her handkerchief. Marco looked around wildly, but he was trapped; there was no escape from wet-eyed, sniffing females.

At least no escape until he was crushed into the narrow pew as his mother elbowed her way past him. 'Oh, Sophie, *grazie, cara.* You performed miracles. Hey, Chesca, this is Sophie, Marco's *ragazza.* Did you see how she transformed Bianca's dress? *Sì, bellissima.*'

His mother kept up her chatter as they made their way down the aisle. She was obviously buzzing from the wedding and wanted everyone to know how Sophie had helped—binding the English girl ever closer to the family, he thought wryly. 'Yes, she and Marco are very close, he's quite besotted,' he heard her confide more than once. 'We expect an announcement any day now.'

Her whispered predictions didn't surprise him, his lack of anger did. But she was wrong; there would be no announcement. Things had moved too fast, so fast he'd barely noticed that they were out of the shallows and heading towards the deep water. Sophie was going home tomorrow and perhaps it was for the best. Enjoy the short time they had left, then put a stop to it before he let her down. He might not mean to, but he would. It was his hallmark after all.

Sophie had been aware of the stares before the wedding started. It was worse than the party at Epiphany. Then, she had been new to the city, unaware of the subtext. Today she knew all too well that everyone was looking at her and wondering if she would be the next Santoro bride. She had been the subject of more than a few cool, assessing once-overs from expensively clad and groomed women, the contemptuous flicker of their eyes judging her and finding her wanting.

But the stares intensified once the ceremony was over. Marco's mother was making it very clear that she considered Sophie one of the family, introducing her to what seemed like every single one of the three hundred guests. Even worse, she told everyone she could about how Sophie had 'saved' Bianca's dress. Sophie knew that if Ashleigh were here she'd be telling her to milk the situation for all she was worth, think of future commissions and suck it up, but she felt guilty taking all the credit—she'd only adapted what was already there after all.

The whole wedding party walked the short distance between the church and the *palazzo* where Bianca and Antonio were hosting their wedding reception. There had, Sophie gathered, been some heated family debate on the venue, the Santoros wanting to hold it at the family home, but Bianca preferring a neutral venue—and for she and Antonio to pick up the tab. 'Mamma wants to control every little detail as it is,' she'd explained to Sophie. 'The only way I can guarantee having things the way I want them is to pay for it myself.'

And goodness knew what she had paid. The couple had taken over one of the most illustrious hotels in Venice for the evening, demanding sole use of the fourteenth-century *palazzo* for their guests. Sophie had been intimidated by the faded glory of the Santoro home, but this fully restored *palazzo* took her breath away, from the bright frescos adorning every wall and ceiling to the marble staircase, the huge terrace overlooking the Grand Canal, furnished with tables, chairs and throws to wrap around the hardier wedding guests venturing out in the January chill, to the ballroom in which the reception was being held. This was an immense room, decorated with elaborate, huge gold frescos, the ceiling high above adding to the feeling of grandeur and space. She had waitressed at some glitzy events over the last eighteen months, had seen some fabulous occasions, but nothing came close to the sheer grandeur of this wedding, this room, this family.

What on earth was she doing here?

'Signorina Bradshaw?' She jumped at a gentle tap on her elbow, turning to see a petite brunette with a wide smile, conservatively dressed in a smart, dark blue suit. 'Hello. I am Flavia, fashion reporter for *Marchesa* magazine.'

That was another unexpected facet to today's wedding. She had known the Santoros were rich, had known that the family was old Venetian blue blood, but it simply hadn't occurred to her that there would be outside interest in the wedding. It came as a shock when she realised several newspapers and magazines had been waiting outside the church and the high society *Marchesa* magazine had permission to cover the early part of the reception. Sophie resisted the urge to smooth down her dress and did her best to smile. 'Hi, yes, I'm Sophie Bradshaw.'

'You are here with Signor Santoro?'

'Erm…yes.' That wasn't exactly privileged information and Marco's mother had already announced it to pretty much the whole of Venice. The reporter looked at her expectantly and Sophie struggled to find something else to say. 'It was very kind of him to ask me along to such a beautiful occasion.'

There, she knew her role was to act as a buffer between Marco and his family's expectations, but at least she wasn't publicly staking her claim. The journalist didn't look convinced, raising a sceptical eyebrow before plastering on her smile. 'The big news is, of course, the wedding dress. Everyone has been raving over it and I hear you are responsible for making some big last-minute changes?'

Sophie paused. She didn't want to say that Bianca had put on weight and she certainly wasn't going to mention the pregnancy. 'I...'

'Sophie saved me.' The bride swooped down upon them, kissing Sophie exuberantly. 'My dress was beautiful, yes, but too plain for such an occasion, not entirely appropriate for a church wedding. And she took this beautiful dress and made it unique and special.' She twirled round, allowing the accompanying photographer to take pictures. 'Look at the stitching, and these beautiful buttons, and how she took it in here and here. She made the dress she's wearing too. Don't be fooled by how simple it looks. It is truly *elegante.*'

To Sophie's relief, once her photo had been taken, one with the bride and one posing self-consciously by herself by one of the three huge windows, the journalist moved away. Sophie scanned the crowds but couldn't see Marco any-where and she couldn't face another round of being introduced as the new member of the family. It was probably a little futile checking her hair and make-up after the magazine had taken her photo, but she knew she needed a few moments to ready herself for the rest of the event.

She'd always found large social events intimidating, much preferring quiet evenings to a big crowd. Make the crowd larger, wealthier and effortlessly chic, add in a language she didn't speak and she was officially way out of her depth.

Luckily it didn't take her long to find the ladies' room. The door led into a large sitting area, filled with inviting-looking seats and sofas and several dressing tables, each piled high with cotton wool, hair spray and even straighteners for maximum primping. A door at the other end led to toilets and sinks and, as another guest came through, Sophie noted the opulence of the marble sinks and the gilt fittings. She suspected the individual toilet stalls might be bigger than her own shower room back in London—not that difficult: most cupboards were bigger than her shower room.

Sinking onto one of the sofas with a sigh of relief, Sophie told herself sternly she had five minutes to get herself together before heading back in. Things were coming to a head, that was all. She was leaving first thing tomorrow—really going this time—and she had to tell Marco about the baby before she did so. He hadn't mentioned anything about seeing each other in London, so she couldn't assume that there would be an easy opportunity to tell him once she was back.

She closed her eyes and wished, just for a moment, that things were different. That she and Marco really were as together as his mother assumed, that she would be joining this loud, overbearing, terrifyingly opinionated, loving, inclusive family. Not once had Sophie felt not good enough. Not when she hadn't known how to address the maid. Not when she couldn't follow the conversation, not when she admitted she made most of her clothes, not when Marco had realised she was worrying about money.

She'd never once felt good enough for Harry. Which was ironic because now she could see she was far, far too good for him.

If she weren't pregnant, would she act any differently? Be more honest about how she felt? It was too difficult to know; she *was* pregnant and although that made everything infinitely more complicated she couldn't be sorry. Besides, Marco's mother was right: she and Marco probably would make a beautiful baby.

Opening her eyes, Sophie jumped. Three terrifyingly elegant women had sat opposite her and were all staring at her in undisguised curiosity. She managed to raise a smile and said, 'Weddings are tiring, aren't they?'

They nodded as if one. All three were wearing their glossy, expensively cut hair down in the kind of swishy style Sophie always envied and were all dressed exquisitely in labels Sophie wasn't sure she'd ever seen outside glossy magazines.

The woman in the middle leaned forward, her eyes bright. 'May I ask you something?' she asked in heavily accented but perfect English.

'I suppose so,' Sophie said warily.

'How did you do it?'

'Do what? Bianca's dress? It was…'

'No,' the woman on the left interrupted her. 'Although that is very impressive. No, how did you tie Marco down?'

'How did I…? I haven't…I mean, we're not engaged.'

'Yet.' With a heavy emphasis. 'I dated him for three years. Mamma was planning my dress, Papà was ready to buy us our own house, and then *poof…*' the woman on the right clicked her fingers '…he was gone. He told me I had trapped him, that he didn't want to be tied down.'

Sophie's stomach lurched. Would he feel the same way when she told him she was pregnant? Trapped?

'I'm sorry to hear that.'

'I was humiliated, heartbroken, and he never told me why. Just left, went to England. Left me to pick up the pieces alone. I should hate him…' Her voice softened. 'I tell myself I hate him…'

'But you…' one of her friends chimed in.

'Everyone is talking about it…'

'Living at the *palazzo*, friends with his sister…'

'What's your secret?'

'I don't know whether to pity or admire you.'

'Or envy you.'

Sophie swallowed. Marco had been completely

up front from the very beginning. He'd told her this was temporary, fun, a one-time thing, but at some point she'd allowed herself to hope for more. There was no point deceiving herself any longer. It wouldn't change anything. She was having his baby; he had to know. Those were the inescapable facts.

'I'm sorry,' she said. 'But I really have to go. If you'll excuse me?'

With a deep breath she got to her feet. It was time to find Marco—whatever happened next was entirely up to him.

CHAPTER TWELVE

MARCO SCANNED THE ROOM. One minute Sophie had been with his sister, the next she had completely disappeared. He was pretty sure she could take care of herself, but in a room that seemed to be comprised solely of his extended family and women he used to date, even the most hardened party-goer would need backup.

Hell, *he* needed backup. That was why she was here, wasn't it?

'Marco.' He jumped as she came up behind him, laying one pale hand on his sleeve.

'There you are. I was thinking you must have been cornered by my great-aunt Annunciata.'

'No, not yet. Look, could I have a word? In private?'

Her hand wasn't the only part of her that was pale. Her cheeks were almost white, her lips bloodless. Anger rose, hot and hungry. Had someone said something to hurt her? 'Is everything okay?'

'Yes, I just need to talk to you about something.'

Marco looked around. The door to the terrace was ajar and it looked as if nobody else was braving the sharp winter air. He took her hand, her fingers sliding into his as if they belonged there, and led her outside. Trees in pots lined the walls and vines twisted around the railings. He selected a table at the far end of the terrace and pulled out a chair for Sophie, tucking one of the blankets left out for the purpose around her shoulders as she sat.

'I was talking to some of the other guests just now. They all knew you.'

'Did they?' He raised his eyebrows. She sounded solemn. Solemn at weddings wasn't usually good.

'One of them was an ex-girlfriend of yours. She's a little bitter. Apparently you practically left her at the altar.'

Understanding dawned. 'You were talking to Celia, which I expect means she was flanked by Beatrice and Elena. They usually work as a team.'

'I didn't get their names.'

Something was off here and he couldn't work out what. 'It's a bit of an exaggeration to say I left her at the altar. We were never formally engaged.'

'So what happened? I deserve to know,' she added. 'If looks could kill, I'd currently be laid out on the floor of the women's bathroom and wedding guests would have to step over my corpse to get to the sinks.'

Marco rubbed his eyes wearily. Celia was so intrinsically mixed up with the events that had led to him leaving Venice, to the row with his father, that he'd done his best to not think of her at all over the last decade. He should have known he couldn't return home without the whole sorry business being dredged up again. 'It sounds like a bigger deal than it was,' he said, staring out at the Grand Canal, following a small open boat with his eyes as it cruised slowly opposite. 'Celia and I started seeing each other after I finished university. We were to-gether for about three years.'

'She said you just disappeared.'

'It wasn't quite like that. She was pretty, a lit-tle crazy, fun, all the things a man in his early twenties finds attractive. I guess I thought I was in love, thought she loved me, not that I had any idea what love was.' Bianca's words floated back to him. She was right; it had been infatu-ation, not love. He sighed. 'She was a welcome distraction from home. I was just starting out, collecting and reselling, developing a client list, building up a reputation, but my father thought I was wasting my time—and told me every chance he got.'

'That must have been difficult.'

'It was challenging,' he admitted. 'But I was young and driven and wanted my own path. I thought Celia agreed with me, but gradually I realised she wanted very different things. She didn't love the Marco Santoro who was passion-ate about his business and happy to start from scratch if he had to. She loved the Santoro heir with all the privileges that entailed and she kept pushing me to listen to my father. To give in.'

'But you didn't.'

'I didn't. So we'd argue, she'd cry, I'd feel guilty, we'd make up. It was an exhausting cycle mirrored by the constant battles with my father. Soon I realised she spent more time at the *palazzo* than I did, that she was shopping with Mamma and going out with Bianca, that she was already considered part of the family. Hints were dropped, more than hints, that a proposal would be nice. Her father took me aside and made noises about buying us a house as a wedding gift. Nonna presented me with her engagement ring and told me how proud I made her.'

Sophie put a cold hand on his. 'That must have been difficult.'

He'd been trapped. Each way he'd turned, an impossible choice. Give in and live a life he didn't want or stand firm and disappoint everyone who loved him. 'My life was just beginning. It should have been full of possibilities. Instead everyone I knew, everyone I loved, everyone I respected was trying to narrow it down, to cage me in. The girl I thought I was falling for had been replaced with a woman I didn't recognise, a woman who didn't want me as I was but wanted to change me, mould me.'

'But she didn't succeed. You walked away.'

Celia had succeeded in one way: she *had* changed him. All that youthful optimism and hope had been replaced with wariness; his home had become a prison.

'I decided I had to leave Venice. I couldn't carry on being scrutinised and criticised at every turn. I told Celia, gave her the option to come with me. She laughed at first, thought I was joking. When she realised I was serious…' He shook his head. 'The contempt in her eyes. I realised then that it was the package she wanted, not the man.'

'She was a fool.'

'She was ambitious. Oh, don't think I spent the next ten years weeping over my lost love. I was relieved more than heartbroken. Besides, it just confirmed what I already knew. That what I was mattered more than who I was and I was tired of it, tired of Venice, tired of all their expectations. So I went to see my father and told him I was done.'

'How did he take it?'

'Not well. He got so angry he collapsed with a suspected heart attack.'

'Oh, Marco.'

'And I went anyway. He was in the hospital and I packed my bags and left. I knew if I stayed the guilt would suck me in and I would never be free, so as soon as the doctors said he should make a full recovery I was out of Venice and starting again. I barely saw him after that, a couple of times a year of guarded pleasantries and then it was too late. For both of us.'

'I'm sure he knew you loved him. I'm sure he was proud of you.'

'Maybe.' Suddenly he was tired of it all. Of the guilt, of the uncertainty. 'All I knew was that I wasn't good enough. Not as a son, as an heir, as a partner. It's been easier—safer—not to get involved. Not to allow anyone to let me down. Allow anyone to look at me and tell me I'm not enough as I am.' Safer but ultimately unsatisfying. Short-term relationships, friendships based on business not deep-rooted companion-ship, family kept at arm's length. No wonder he'd worked eighteen hours a day, seven days a week. He'd had very little else.

He looked at Sophie as she stared out onto the Grand Canal, her profile sad and thoughtful, and for a moment he wondered what would happen if she told him he did matter, he mattered to her. Would he be able to believe her—or would he brush her off, turn away?

Time stood still, the air shimmering over the water while he waited an eternity for her to speak. She swallowed, a convulsive shudder, and her hand pressed on his, icy now in the winter chill.

'I don't believe you're not enough, Marco, at least I hope you are, more than enough. Not for me, I know that's not what you want, but for your child. I'm pregnant, Marco. I'm having a baby, your baby.'

CHAPTER THIRTEEN

SHE COULDN'T LOOK him straight in the eye.
Instead Sophie stared at her hand, still covering his, gleaming pale white in the moonlight,
and waited. Marco had stilled under her touch,
turning to marble the second the words left her
mouth.

'Pregnant?'

'Yes.' She waited for him to ask the obvious
questions. *Are you sure? How do I know it's
mine?* But they didn't come. Relief flooded over
her as he nodded slowly.

Only to recede as he looked straight over at
her, eyes hooded. 'Then we had better get married.'

It wasn't a question.

It was an assumption. Sophie's heart sped up.
'Married?'

'London would be best. Three weeks from

now. We'll tell everyone we wanted to keep it quiet. We don't want this kind of fuss.' He shrugged in a way that encompassed all of Bianca's wedding.

No, Sophie didn't need three hundred guests, had no desire to book out an exclusive old *palazzo*, say her vows in a world-famous church. But when—if—she got married she would want her friends, her family there. She would want it to be a celebration of love, just as Bianca was so clearly celebrating her love for Antonio today. Not a clandestine affair hidden from the world as if she were ashamed.

And if—when—she got married she wanted to be asked. She didn't need an extravagant proposal, but she would hope that any future husband wouldn't just *assume*…

'Marco, I…'

'Then we'll return here. You can live at the *palazzo*. You'll need family around you and you don't want to go back to Manchester. Besides, I need to be either here or London, so it has to be Venice. I can sell the London house, get a flat for when I'm there. I will have to travel a great deal, another reason why you'll need my family close by.'

That was how he saw her future, was it? Here in Venice, safely tucked away with his family, the family he'd spent over ten years avoiding as much as possible, while he stayed in London.

She opened her mouth, but he ploughed on. 'I don't think we should tell anyone anything yet. You can go back to London as planned tomorrow. I'll be back in a week. I'll arrange for somebody to move your things into my house this week.'

It was obviously all decided. All taken care of in less than a minute's decision-making. It didn't matter what she thought, what she wanted. She was a problem to be taken care of. A problem he had solved in record time.

It wasn't that she didn't love Venice, that she couldn't imagine living here, although she wasn't sure she would ever feel at home in the huge, ancient *palazzo*. It wasn't that she didn't adore Marco's family, overbearing as they were, because she did. But it had taken Sophie far too long to get to the point where *she* made the decisions about her life. She wasn't about to hand over control to someone else. Just go along meekly with his plans like an obedient little wife.

'Marco, stop. We don't need to decide all this now.' She couldn't help the slight emphasis on the 'we'. 'Let's take a few days to think about it and talk about it then, when you've had time to digest everything.'

He got to his feet, body half turned away, the message clear; this conversation was over. 'There's nothing to decide. Look, Sophie, you might not like it. You don't have to like it. This doesn't fit my plans either.' Hurt lanced through her at his cold tones, at each distinct word. 'But what's done is done and we need to act like adults, put our own preferences aside.' He smiled then, a wintry half-smile that left her colder than his earlier bleakness. 'We get on well enough. We have chemistry. There are worse foundations for marriage.'

'Yes, but there are better foundations too.' She looked up at him, putting every ounce of conviction she had into her voice. 'Marco, it's the twenty-first century. We can both be involved, be good parents without needing to be married. We don't need to live together, or even *be* together. We just need to respect each other and work together. I need you to listen to me, to consult me, not to make pronouncements that affect my entire life and expect me to jump to.' Sophie could hear the quiver in her voice and swallowed, holding back the threatened tears. 'I know you don't want to get married and so thank you for suggesting it. But I don't think a reluctant marriage is the best thing for me or for the baby.'

She stood up, the blanket slipping off her shoulders as she did so. 'I am heading back to the *palazzo*. Please make my apologies to Bianca. I'm going to get my plane tomorrow and I'm asking you to give me some space. Please don't come to my room tonight or offer to drop me off in the morning—I think we both need some time to think. Think about what's best for *all* of us.'

Head held high, she touched him lightly on the cheek before turning and walking away. She'd been expecting anger or denial. Not this cold acceptance. But secretly, buried so deep down she'd hardly been aware of it, she'd been hoping for more. Maybe not love, she wasn't that much of a fool, but liking. An indication he wanted to be with her. Not cold, hard duty.

But it looked as if cold, hard duty was all he had to offer—and it wasn't enough. She deserved more—even if her heart was breaking as she turned and walked away. But better a cracked heart now than a lifetime with someone who didn't want or respect her. Better a cracked heart than allowing someone to dictate her life. Because she'd allowed that to happen twice, and she'd had to fight to be free twice. Last time she'd vowed never again and she'd meant it. She meant it now. No matter how much it hurt.

CHAPTER FOURTEEN

'I CAN'T BELIEVE there are so many photos of you. It's like Marco and his family are famous!' Ashleigh was once again searching through Italian gossip sites on Sophie's laptop.

'Not famous exactly, it's just they're a really old family. A really old rich family. A bit like minor royalty.' Sophie turned her head, not wanting to catch a glimpse of Marco, even on screen. He hadn't texted, hadn't called. A week of radio silence. She'd asked for time, asked for space, but this was beginning to feel a lot like punishment. 'Marco and Bianca are gossip-column staples. Her wedding was a big deal. Not that I knew that when I offered to fix her dress. I'd have been far too terrified.'

'So that makes you the mother-to-be of minor royalty,' Grace said.

'I can't believe you're pregnant.' Emma was

staring at Sophie's stomach. 'You haven't put on an ounce.'

'I have, many ounces, but half of it is Italian food,' Sophie pointed out, but Emma's words brought her situation home. It was too easy, back in the safety of her flat, of her routine, to hide from her future. But that future was growing rapidly and she couldn't hide it for much longer. 'And I can't believe it either. There are moments when I'm thrilled—and then I start panicking again. I don't know how to be a mother. It's not like I have the best relationship with mine.'

'Sure you know how,' Ashleigh said with a soft smile. 'You know how to be an awesome friend. You're over halfway there.'

'Besides...' Emma jumped to her feet and stepped over to give her a hug. Sophie leaned gratefully on her shoulder, glad of the support. 'You have us. We're going to be the best team of aunties-stroke-fairy-godmothers any child ever had. You're not alone, Soph. Don't ever think it.'

'And I wouldn't worry about your future. I predict amazing things,' Grace said, wrestling the laptop away from Ashleigh. 'Not only is the whole of Italy wild about the alterations you made to Bianca's dress, but they love the going-away outfit you made her too. I've seen dozens of blogs and articles raving about it. Now your website is finally going live...' she shot a mock stern look at Sophie '...and people can actually *order* your clothes, success can't be far away.'

'Long-deserved success,' Ashleigh chimed in, holding up her cup of tea in a toast.

Sophie blinked back tears. Not only had her friends collected her from the airport, smothered her with affection, tea and cake, waited patiently until she had been able to find the words to tell them about the baby—and about Marco and her feelings for him—but they had also gently encouraged her to capitalise on her new-found design fame, helping her put the finishing touches to her website and testing it for her so when it went live—any second now—she could be confident it worked. Ashleigh had also helped her organise her space in the tiny flat so that finished designs could be photographed in a clutter-free space and her material was neatly stacked, giving her more room to work. Potential customers could either choose from her small collection of existing stock or order by design, choosing the material they liked best from her assortment of vintage prints or sending their own for her to make up.

One day she would like to have a larger collection of ready-to-buy stock—but for that she would need a studio and storage, possibly a couple of seamstresses. No, tiny steps were best. If she could just make enough to keep herself and the baby afloat, then she would have options; she didn't want to need Marco's money. She *would* like his emotional support though.

Which was ironic—he had money to spare but support, real support, was much harder for him. Maybe too hard.

'Right, we have to get off.' Ashleigh hauled herself to her feet. 'Are you sure you don't want to come, Sophie?' Grace's fiancé was hosting a glamorous fundraising event at his hotel and all three of her friends were attending. Funny to think that just a few months ago they would probably have all been waitressing for it.

Which reminded her, she needed to discuss

hours and jobs with Clio. Heavy cleaning and too much standing around were probably out, but Sophie wanted to ensure she had some steady income while the first orders came in. Her waitressing days weren't behind her yet.

'I'm sure. I'm exhausted by nine at the moment. Besides, I want to stalk my inbox and wait for an order.'

'It won't be long,' Grace said loyally, dropping a kiss onto her cheek. 'If you need a hand, well, I can't sew. Or cut out. But I am very good at parcels—and making tea.'

'You'll be my first port of call,' Sophie promised, kissing her back and then embracing Emma and Ashleigh in turn.

The flat felt larger without her friends—a little larger—and a lot emptier. Sophie put her laptop on the kitchen counter and refreshed her email. Nothing. Maybe her friends were wrong, maybe the publicity and excitement over Bianca's wedding dress and the two-piece, sixties-inspired going-away outfit she had gifted the bride were just a storm in a teacup and wouldn't translate into sales.

But she couldn't believe that, wouldn't believe it. After all, photos of Bianca were everywhere and not just in the Italian press; a few British sites had picked up the chatter about the 'London-based designer' and had run short pieces extolling her as one to watch. Every piece used the same photo, taken at the wedding, Sophie in her grey dress smiling up at Marco, handsome in his tuxedo. Her heart turned over at the picture. They looked so happy, so together—to a casual observer as if they were head over heels in love. But she wasn't a casual observer.

Impatient to shake her bad mood, Sophie grabbed her pad and pencil. The success of Bianca's wedding dress made her wonder if there might be more bridal commissions in her future and she wanted to be prepared...

Stretching, she realised she'd lost track of time. Over two hours had passed while she'd sketched her first attempts at twenties-, fifties- and sixties-inspired bridal gowns. Not too bad, she decided, standing back and taking a fresh look. She'd like to get some samples started soon, a heavy silk for the twenties dress, lace and chiffon for the fifties dress and embroidered velvet for the sixties-inspired design.

As she moved the pad further away her hand knocked the keyboard and her laptop screen blared into life, opening onto her brand-new inbox. Only, it wasn't empty as it had been when she last looked; no, there were four un-opened emails sitting there and they didn't look like spam... With a trembling hand she clicked on one and scanned the message; would she be able to design a wedding dress and what were her fees?

Sophie took a deep breath; she'd been right to turn her attentions to bridal. The second was from a boutique here in Chelsea asking if they could discuss stocking some of her designs, the third another enquiry, this time for an evening gown. So far so good. No actual money but the possibility of work. The fourth, however, came from the automated payment system she had set up. She took a deep breath and clicked. 'Yes!' she shouted. 'Yes!' An order, a real order for two of her dresses, a shift dress in a polka-dot pink and a copy of the dress she'd worn to Bianca's wedding in a gorgeous green flowered cotton. She had done it! She was a real designer with real sales to people she didn't know.

She looked round, wanting to jump up and down, to babble her excitement into someone else's ear, to have someone else to confirm that, yes, the emails said exactly what she thought they said. But there was nobody there; her shoebox had never felt so spacious, never felt so lonely. She could text her friends, of course. They would be delighted. But, she realised, sinking back onto her stool, the euphoria draining away, she didn't want to impress them. She didn't need to witness their reactions.

She wanted Marco there, celebrating alongside her. She wanted to see him look impressed, to tell her how proud he was. But he was a long, long way away. Emotionally, physically, in every way that mattered. She'd thought she'd been lonely in the past, but it didn't compare to how she felt now. Completely and utterly alone. She couldn't let that stop her. She'd pulled herself back from the brink before, she could do it again. Besides, it wasn't all about her, not any more. She had to be strong for the baby—she simply had no other option.

Marco took another look at the address. He hadn't thought too much about where Sophie lived, but he'd assumed it would be in a flat in one of Chelsea's leafy streets, possibly sharing with a couple of friends. Not on this noisy, busy road, cars honking horns impatiently as they queued three abreast, fumes acrid in the damp air.

'Number one eight one,' he muttered, coming to a stop outside the right building. There was a takeaway on the ground floor and Marco grimaced as the scent of greasy fried chicken assailed him. The door to the flats was a dingy green, the doorstop covered in thrown-away boxes and discarded chicken bones. No way was any child of his growing up here, he vowed.

He scanned the names, almost illegible against the long list of buzzers, but before he found Sophie's name, the door opened and a young woman barged out, leaving the door ajar. Marco added security to the list of undesirables and shouldered it open. He needed Flat Ten. He looked at the door at the end of the ground floor—number one. It looked like he was going up…and up and up. Another item for his list: too many stairs. How on earth did she think she would cart a baby up here?

It was easier to list all the reasons for Sophie to move than it was to face the other list, the list that had brought him to the door. The list that started with how big, how lonely his bed felt every night, the list that included how much he missed her. The list that concluded that he didn't want to live in the Chelsea house or Venice on his own. The list that told him he had reacted badly to the news of her pregnancy, that he might be a little too convinced of his own eligibility, possibly bordering on arrogant where his marriage prospects were concerned. He patted Nonna's ring, secure in his top pocket. He would do better this time. He had to.

Finally he made his way to the top floor. Sophie's door was the same dull navy as all the other flat doors, but the handle was polished and two terracotta pots filled with lush greenery brightened the narrow landing. Marco shifted, nervous for the first time since he had boarded the plane this morning fired up with purpose. Before he could start listing why this was a bad idea he raised his hand and knocked firmly at the door.

'Mr Kowaski, have you forgotten your keys again? It's okay, I... Oh.' The door was fully open and Sophie stood there, shock mingling with something Marco couldn't define but hoped might be pleasure. 'How did you get in?'

'A neighbour.'

'They're not supposed to just let people... Not that it matters. Come on in.'

She stepped back and Marco entered her flat. There wasn't much of it, a small attic room, a large dormer window to the right the only natural light. A sofa ran along the wall to his left, opposite him a narrow counter defined the small kitchen, a high table barely big enough for two by the window. He'd been on larger boats.

The furniture was old and battered, but the room was scrupulously clean, the cream walls covered in bright prints and swathes of material, the sofa heaped with inviting throws and cushions. Along the wall adjoining the window a clothing rail lined up, dresses hanging on it in a neat row and drawings and patterns were pinned up on a huge easel.

There was no door between the living space and her bedroom, just a narrow archway. Through it he could see a single bed and two more rails bulging with brightly patterned dresses and skirts.

He walked over to the nearest rail and pulled out the first dress. Just like the outfit she'd worn to Bianca's wedding—just like everything he'd seen her in—it was deceptively simple. She obviously took her inspiration from the past, each outfit having a vintage vibe, but the detailing and cut gave it a modern twist.

'So this is what you do.' She'd said she wanted to be a designer, he'd seen her work first-hand, but he hadn't appreciated just how talented— just how motivated—she was, not until he stood in the tiny flat, more workspace than home. He'd met so many Chelsea girls over the last few years, women with family money who pottered around playing at being designers or artists or jewellers. He'd assumed Sophie belonged to their tribe, although looking back the signs were there: how careful she was with money, how little she spoke about her family. It was painfully clear how much he'd misjudged her, how little he knew about her.

'This is what I do. It's taken me a long time to get even this far. I don't make a living from it yet. In fact...' she took a deep breath '...I owe you an apology. I didn't mean to mislead you...'

'About what?'

'When we met, that first night. I was at the party but not as a guest. You didn't see me because I was invisible—I was waitressing there. I was supposed to be waitressing at the Snowflake Ball as well. Only, my friends played fairy godmother and bought me a ticket. That's how I make ends meet, have done since I moved to London. I work for Maids in Chelsea, cleaning, shopping, bar work—whatever is needed.'

Her blue eyes were defiant, her chin tilted, hands bunched on her hips. 'You worked and produced all this? When did you find time to sleep? To eat?'

The defiance dimmed, replaced with relief. 'Sleep's overrated.'

'You didn't lie. You told me you were a designer. Looking at all this, I'd say that's exactly what you are. These are incredible.'

'Thank you.' She twisted her hands together. 'But you didn't come here to pay me compliments. I know we need to talk, but it's late and I'm really tired. Could we meet tomorrow and do this then?'

She did look exhausted, he realised with a pang of guilt. Purple shadows darkened her eyes, her hair, twisted up into a loose ponytail was duller than usual, her lips pale. She looked more vulnerable than he'd ever seen her and he ached for the right to take care of her. She was carrying his child. *His.* It was almost impossible to imagine, her body still slender, seemingly unchanged, and yet his blood thrilled at the realisation. He'd been running from this commitment for so long yet now he was confronted with the actuality he was filled with a primal joy. A determination to do better, be a better father than he had been a son, to not make the same mistakes his own father had made but to love his child no matter what their aspirations, who they wanted to be.

'We can, but I just need to say one thing. I'm sorry for how I reacted, when you told me about the pregnancy. It was such a shock, so unexpected. I needed to fix it, solve it. That's what I do.'

'I understand.'

'I made assumptions about you, about us. That was wrong. But I've missed you, Sophie. All this week I keep turning to speak to you, to see your reaction, and you're not there. That's my fault, I know, and it's up to me to make things right.' It was his turn to take a deep breath. He had never thought he would ever reach this point, but now he was here it made sense as nothing had ever made sense before. Maybe this was destined, the meeting in the snow, the baby, bringing him to this point.

Reaching into his top pocket, he pulled out the small black box. Sophie's eyes widened and she retreated back a step, but he took her hand in his, sinking to one knee like an actor playing his part. 'Sophie, it would make me very happy if you would do me the very great honour of becoming my wife.'

He smiled up at her, waiting for her agreement.

'No. I'm sorry, Marco, but I can't.'

CHAPTER FIFTEEN

SOPHIE STEPPED BACK one more step, pulling her hand free of his. A chill of loneliness shivered through her and she had to fight the urge to tell him she'd changed her mind, of course she would marry him. But he wasn't here for her, not for Sophie Bradshaw, he was here for the mother of his child. Here because it was the right thing to do. And she appreciated that, she really did. But she couldn't stake the rest of her life on it. 'I'm sorry,' she repeated.

Marco slowly straightened, regret mingled with anger and embarrassment clear on his face. 'I see.'

Ten minutes ago all Sophie had wanted was the coolness of her newly washed sheets, to burrow under her duvet and fall into the kind of heavy, dreamless, all-encompassing sleep her body demanded. She'd asked him to wait until tomorrow, told him she was tired and yet he'd still overridden her wishes. The only difference from last week's conversation was that this time Marco had couched his demand for marriage as a request.

A request he clearly expected her to acquiesce to.

No, nothing had changed. 'I appreciate that you think getting married is the right thing to do, especially knowing how you feel about marriage, but I can't.'

Eyes grim, mouth narrowed, he nodded once. 'Then there's nothing else to say.' Marco turned, clearly heading for the door, out of her flat and potentially out of her life. Out of their child's life.

Sophie wavered, torn. She wanted him involved, but he expected so much, too much. But, dammit, she knew she owed him an explanation; after all, it wasn't his fault it wasn't enough for her. At least a dozen women at the wedding would have leapt at his first decisive statement; they'd have swooned at a ring and a bended knee—after saying yes, of course. 'Would you like a drink? I think I have a beer in the fridge.'

He stilled, stopped. 'That would be nice, but you're tired.'

'I am, but you're here now. Sit down.' She nodded at the sofa. 'I'll bring you a beer.'

Sophie busied herself for a few minutes, opening the beer, making herself a peppermint tea and pouring some crisps into a bowl and setting it on the tiny portable all-purpose table, before sinking into the sofa next to him. Next to him but not touching. She pulled her legs up before her, propping her chin on her knees, her arms hugging her legs, wanting the warmth, the support. Neither spoke, the silence neither hostile nor comfortable, more a cautious truce.

'I owe you an honest explanation, at the very least,' she said after a while. 'It's not easy for me to talk about, even to think about. I'm not very proud of my past.'

His eyes flickered at that, but he didn't say anything. Instead he took a long drink from the bottle of beer and settled back against the sofa, his gaze steady as he watched her. Sophie stared past him, her eyes fixed on the wall behind him, tracing the colours in the material hanging there, following the pattern round and round.

'For most of my life I thought my only value was in how happy I made others. My parents weren't cruel, not at all. I had everything. Private school, lovely clothes, everything I needed except for freedom, except for autonomy. My mother liked a project, you see. She's very determined, very focussed.' She smiled. 'I often wonder what will happen when she meets your mother. They'll be the definition of the unstoppable force versus the immoveable object. Scientists should study them under test conditions.'

She sipped her tea, her gaze still fixed on the material. It was hard to untangle her feelings about her mother; they were so complicated. She'd been so loved, Sophie knew that. But the burden of expectation had been crushing and Sophie wasn't sure she'd ever stop being resentful, stop wishing for a more carefree childhood. A childhood that had prepared her for adulthood instead of leaving her wide open and vulnerable.

'I think I mentioned before that I was born quite a long time after my brothers. It was like being an only child in many ways and I was quite isolated. My mum liked to pick out my friends, my clothes, my activities, and I soon learned that my role in the family was to make her happy—and she was happy when I did exactly what she wanted. It's dangerous, linking love to approval, making a child feel that it's conditional. And that was very much how I felt. I didn't dare complain, I didn't dare disagree because when I had her approval I knew I was loved. But I wasn't happy. My school was quite a long way away from my home and I was dancing most evenings from a young age, so I didn't have many friends. Ashleigh was my closest friend, but I only knew her for a short while and then her family moved back to Australia. By the time I hit my mid-teens I was a bit of a loner and really naïve.

'My mother had planned for me to apply for professional training when I was sixteen—but I think I told you in Venice that my heart wasn't in it. It was the first time I had said no, first time I'd let her down and she didn't hide her disappointment in me. But I felt free for the first time.

I started to go out, to gigs to see local bands, to make my own clothes and find my own look. The more I started to work out who I wanted to be, the harder she tried to hold on. We had such terrible, horrible rows, said nasty, vicious things.'

They had both been guilty, she knew that. But Sophie had still been a child in many ways and her mother had left her in no doubt that she wasn't good enough, not any more. That Sophie's own style, her own wishes, her own hobbies were wrong and behind her bravado her fledgling self-confidence had begun to crumble.

'That was a long time ago. How are things now?'

'Fragile,' she admitted. 'Uncomfortable. That's why I rarely go back to Manchester.' She found a smile. 'See, we do have some things in common.' But their solutions to their family problems had been drastically different. Marco had taken control of his life, made a huge success out of his passions, his business. Sophie? She had run from one controlling situation to another.

She took another sip of the comforting tea and

tried to order her thoughts. She hadn't spoken about Harry since the day she had finally come to her senses and walked out of the door. If she told Marco, it would be like probing a wound to see if it had really healed or still bubbled with infection.

'Like I said, I was a bit of a loner and really naïve. Ripe to be exploited. I met Harry at one of his gigs. He was the singer—all brash confidence and raw sexuality. I had never seen or spoken to anybody like him before and I was besotted before we even spoke. When he singled me out I thought I was the luckiest girl alive. It was every teen cliché come true. My parents hated him, of course. He was older than me for a start, arrogant, entitled. Looking back, he was just really rude, but I thought he was authentic and being true to himself. The more they tried to stop me seeing him, the more attractive he got.'

'How old were you?'

'Seventeen, a really young seventeen. I thought I was Juliet, of course, brimful of forbidden love.' Her mouth twisted into a wry smile. 'There is nothing more guaranteed to drive your hormonal teenaged daughter into the arms of a complete sod than to try to stop her seeing him. If they'd relaxed and made him welcome, or at least pretended to, maybe I'd have seen the truth a lot sooner.'

Maybe.

'Things were tense for a year. Home was like a battlefield, every sentence an ambush. My parents couldn't cope. Their sweet, biddable daughter had been replaced by a foul-mouthed hellion. I drank, stayed out all night, ditched school—and of course Harry encouraged me all the way. It shouldn't be an excuse, but, remember, I needed approval to feel loved and Harry's approval was intoxicating. I lived for it—and he knew it. Eventually my dad put his foot down in a "not in my house, young lady, you live in these walls you obey my rules" kind of way and I said "fine". Packed my bags and walked out the day I turned eighteen.'

He echoed her thoughts. 'We're both runaways, then. You're right, we do have something in common.'

'Only, you moved to a new city and started a

successful business. I moved into a squat three miles away and became a cook, cleaner, cheerleader and paid heavily for the privilege. Harry had me exactly where he wanted me. My original plan had been to go to college and study art and textiles while living with him, but he persuaded me I'd be wasting my time. That I wasn't that talented, that original.' To her horror she could feel the tears gathering in her eyes and swiped her sleeve angrily against them. 'He said I'd be of more use getting a job so we could get a flat—obviously he was too busy being a musician to dirty his hands with real work. So instead of college I worked in a greasy spoon café. I was there for six years. I paid for our flat and our food. I cleaned our flat. I cooked our food. I soon learned not to ask Harry to do anything, not to expect anything from him. Including fidelity.'

She swiped her eyes again. 'I know what you're thinking because I'm thinking it too. Why did I put up with it? Why did I let him treat me that way? I think it every day. He made me feel like I was completely worthless, that I couldn't do anything, be anyone without him. That I was lucky to have him. And I believed him. The worst part is that every now and then he'd do something sweet, remind me why I fell in love with him in the first place. I lived for those moments, craved them, would lie there every night he didn't come home and relive every one of them.'

His hands had curled into fists and a primal part of him welcomed his anger. 'He didn't deserve you. You know that, right? You left, you got away.'

'Eventually. We were at a wedding and when he saw the head bridesmaid his tongue was practically hanging out. I'd turned a blind eye to his flings before, but when he kissed her on the dance floor—in front of his friends and family—I knew I had to get out before he destroyed me completely. I called a taxi, packed my things and went straight to the train station. I didn't trust myself not to waver if I saw him.'

'That was very brave.'

'I was running on adrenaline,' she admitted. 'If I'd thought about what I was doing, moving on my own to a city I didn't know, to a place where I knew no one, I would have just given up.'

But he was shaking his head. 'You're stronger than you think, Sophie. When I look at you I don't see a victim or weakness. I see a survivor. I see resilience. I see strength.'

Warmth flooded through her, not just because of his words but because of the respect she saw in his eyes. 'It's been a slow journey, Marco. I don't feel strong, not all the time. I've worked really hard to get to this place. My flat is tiny and horribly overpriced, but *I* pay the rent for me. It's my home, my sanctuary. I've finally put my designs out in the world. I have friends here, good friends. I'm my own person.'

'You'd still be your own person if you married me. I wouldn't stand in your way.'

She would give anything to believe him—but she didn't. 'When I told you about the baby you went into decision-making overdrive. We would do this, I would do that, this is how it would be. I know you were thinking of me and the baby, but I can't live like that, Marco, not again.'

He had paled, his eyes hard. 'You think I'm

like your ex? That I would control you? Put you down?'

'No, no…' She reached a hand out to him. 'You're nothing like Harry. Your kindness was one of the first things I lo…liked about you. But you do like things your own way. That's why you moved to London in the first place. You're used to being in charge and I won't risk losing myself. I won't be the peacemaker, the compromiser again. I can't.'

She needed him to understand, desperately hoped that he did, but his mouth was grim.

'I understand, Sophie, I really do. But this isn't just about you, not any more. You might not like it, but my role now is to take care of you and our baby and I won't let you push me aside. You've come a long way, but you need to learn to let go, to trust me not to hurt you.'

She opened her mouth to tell him she did, but she couldn't say the words. He sighed. 'There's a difference between protecting you and controlling you. I have to do the first, but I can promise you I'll never do the second. I'm here, Sophie, for you and for our baby and I'm not going anywhere. The sooner you accept that, the better. Thanks for the drink. I'll see myself out.'

She sat frozen as he got to his feet. Two seconds later the door clicked behind him and he was gone. Part of her was relieved he still wanted to be involved, that she wouldn't have to bring the baby up alone, but his parting words rang in her ears. *The sooner you accept that, the better.* He was wrong; she wasn't accepting anything and no man would ever tell her what she could or could not do ever again. 'Damn you, Marco,' she whispered as she got wearily to her feet, the cold bone deep inside her. 'Why didn't you ask me what I want rather than telling me what you think I need?'

He said he respected her, now she needed him to show it. It was a poor substitute for love, but Sophie suspected it was all she was going to get. The question was, would it be enough?

CHAPTER SIXTEEN

'ARE YOU SURE you don't want me to come with you? Hold your hand?'

Sophie smiled, touched at the concern in Ashleigh's voice. 'It's a scan. I don't think it hurts.'

'That's not the point,' her friend said firmly. 'It's a huge moment, and on Valentine's Day too. You're going to need someone to hold the tissues.'

'I'm not dragging you away from Lukas on your first Valentine's Day. What kind of best friend do you think I am? Besides, it's different for you loved-up types, but I've never made a fuss about the fourteenth of February. It's just a day.'

Ashleigh's voice took on the dreamy tinge she always used when talking about Lukas. 'I think Lukas is planning dinner in Paris from all the not so subtle hints, but we can get a later train. I don't mind at all.'

'No, go to Paris, be happy and in love. I'll email you a picture of the scan, okay?'

'Only if you're sure.'

'More than sure. Now go and get ready to look surprised. *Au revoir.*'

'Email me straight away, love you.'

'I love you too.' Sophie clicked her phone off and suppressed a sigh. It would have been lovely to have her oldest and best friend with her when she met her baby for the first time, but there was no way she would butt in on Ashleigh's first Valentine's Day with Lukas.

She turned her phone over and over in her hand. She didn't *have* to go alone. After all, there was someone else who was probably just as keen to meet his baby. Their baby.

She hadn't met up with Marco at all over the last few weeks, partly because he was travelling and partly because he seemed to be respecting her request for space and time. It hadn't stopped him sending details through for potential flats and houses he 'wondered' if she might find more suitable or arranging a delivery service to supply her with home-cooked meals she just needed to heat up. She told herself that she should be mad at his officiousness, but she was so busy and tired the meals were a godsend and she couldn't help but concede he had a point about the flat. Hers was too small, too noisy and up too many flights of stairs.

The only problem was that every property he sent her was way, way out of her price range. She was pretty sure he was expecting to pay for wherever she moved to and knew that unless she suddenly sold every outfit she had made she was going to have to accept in the short-term at least. Necessity didn't make it easy though. 'For goodness' sake,' she told herself. 'At least he's not expecting you to support him. That's a huge improvement, right?' But much as it made sense it still felt like the first step on a very slippery slope.

She sighed. They did need to talk and a scan was a good, positive place to start. Before she could change her mind she called up his name and pressed Send. It was the right thing to do.

* * *

'Buongiorno.'

Marco scanned Sophie with a critical eye, nodding with satisfaction as he noted the shadows had disappeared from under her eyes and her cheeks had colour once more. Her hair was freshly washed and full of its usual bounce and her eyes no longer had the sad, defeated look he'd taken away with him when he'd left her a few weeks ago. 'You look beautiful.'

'Hi.' She smiled shyly at him and his heart squeezed. It had taken every single ounce of self-control he possessed not to call her or pop round over the last few weeks, but he had promised her, promised himself, that he would give her the control she needed, the time she needed. It had seemed like an eternity.

He'd thought he'd missed her when she left Italy, but that was nothing to the way he'd felt over the last few weeks. He'd thrown himself into work, but it had been almost impossible to concentrate when all he could think about was how he had blown it, how he had destroyed the best thing that had ever happened to him. Through arrogance, through ignorance.

Marco wasn't sure when he had fallen in love with Sophie, but he did know that this pain in his chest, the ache in his heart, the constant knowledge that something fundamental was missing, was love. He suspected he had fallen for her at some point in Venice. He was sure he loved her when he'd walked away from her flat, when he knew he'd let her down and had no idea how to fix it. When he'd decided that he had to respect her decisions, her choices, no matter how much it hurt him to do so.

He'd hoped that it would simplify things, but, looking at her nervous smile, he realised it complicated everything. If he told her how he felt, he suspected she would feel manipulated, think that he was saying what she wanted to hear, not what he felt, and after the last few weeks he wouldn't blame her.

He usually had all the answers, but today he had nothing. 'Thank you, for asking me here today.'

'I should have given you more notice. It's lucky you were in London.'

He hadn't left London, although he'd given her the impression he was away. He couldn't have left her if his business depended on it. What if she needed him and he was nowhere to be found? He'd let down one family member through pride. That was more than enough.

'I'd have found a way to get here. What do we do now?'

'We go in there, register, I have to drink lots of water and then we meet our baby. Ready?'

Our baby. The words hit him with full force. He, Marco Santoro, was going to be a father. Excitement mingled with pride filled him and he vowed he would do anything and everything to keep his child safe and secure. To make him or her happy. For the first time he understood why his mother fretted and planned and pressured him. Why his father had insisted he knew best no matter what Marco said or felt. They too felt this way; misguided as they might have been, they had just wanted to protect him. He just needed to remember that his version of happiness might not be the same as his child's. He took a deep breath. Yes, he was ready for father-hood and all it entailed. '*Sì*, let's do this.'

'I can't believe this is our child.' Marco took another look at the black-and-white picture in disbelief.

'I know, it does look a little like an alien, doesn't it? Do you think I got beamed up onto a spaceship and just didn't realise it?'

'Shh, the *bambino* will hear you. An alien in-deed.' He snorted. 'With that nose? This is a Ve-netian baby for sure.'

'The next scan we can get in colour, you can properly see features and everything. Did you mind that they didn't tell us the sex? We could go for a private scan if you wanted to find out.'

Hope flared at her casual use of 'we'. 'I don't mind either way. Do you want to know?'

'Yes and no,' she admitted. 'It would be handy for names, but I'm not really a pink for a girl, blue for a boy type. I just want it to be healthy and happy.'

'It will be.' He knew he sounded serious, but

he would lay his life down for that little alien without even blinking.

They'd reached the hospital doors and Sophie paused. 'I know you're busy, but do you have to get back? I'm really grateful you've given me some time, but there's a lot of things we need to talk about. It's all feeling very real at the moment.'

'I can clear my diary.' He already had, but she didn't need to know that. 'Where do you want to go?'

'Anywhere outside. It's so nice to have a dry day after two weeks of rain, I want to take advantage of it.'

Marco agreed. The torrential downpours of the last two weeks had added to his impatience as he'd waited for Sophie to get in touch.

'I could eat though,' she added. 'Before I kept eating to stop me feeling sick. Now I just want to eat all the time because I am ravenous. The books tell me I need to be really healthy, but my body just wants carbs, the greasier and unhealthier, the better. You can tell the baby is half Italian the amount of pasta and pizza it demands.'

'I think I know just the place.' He hesitated. 'Unless you have somewhere in mind?'

'No, go ahead. And while we're talking about food, thank you for arranging for those meals. There have been times when I was too tired to even make toast. They have been brilliant.'

Marco exhaled. Bianca had announced her pregnancy shortly after he'd last seen Sophie and had mentioned how tired she was in the evening and what an effort making dinner was. The difference was she had Mamma taking around dishes of pasta and Antonio to cook for her; he'd hated to think of Sophie exhausted and hungry all alone. 'So the meals come under protective and not controlling?'

She nodded. 'They do. They also come under thoughtful and sweet. I really appreciate it.'

It was a start. If he had his way, she'd be living with him and wouldn't need to cope on her own. But he had agreed to respect her wishes—it didn't mean he couldn't make things a little easier for her though.

Marco hailed a cab the second they left the hospital and gave directions as he opened the door for Sophie. Neither of them spoke as the taxi crawled along. It was barely three miles to their destination, but in London traffic that could mean an eternity. As they sat there Marco was assailed by homesickness for the city of his birth. Yes, Venice could be insanely crowded, but just five minutes on a boat and he could be in a deserted spot the tourists would never discover. London had been a wonderful adventure, the place where he had grown up, established himself, become a man in his own right, not just the Santoro heir, but he was ready to move on.

Except Sophie was here—and so his child would be here. Which meant London was his home too for the foreseeable future.

'I don't know this area at all.' Sophie was looking around as the taxi inched its way around Hyde Park heading north. 'I spent my first few nights in London at a cheap hotel near Euston while I looked for work and, once I had the job, rented a flat as close by the office as I could afford. Luckily I had a small savings account I'd kept from Harry—if he'd known, he'd have spent it on guitars or booze or a lads' holiday. I was saving up for a wedding or a baby. Luckily I came to my senses before either of those chained me to him, but it did mean I could afford the first six months' rent while I started to make a life for myself here. But I'm ashamed to say I haven't explored London much at all in the year and a half I've been here. I'm usually working for Clio or working for myself at home.'

She sounded so matter of fact, Marco couldn't imagine how hard it must have been starting afresh in a new city where she knew no one, had nothing. He had already had some contacts when he'd made the move over, a fledgling business and money enough to make the move easy and comfortable. Being his own man was so important to him, but, he acknowledged ruefully, it was easier to start from a position of privilege with a network of contacts than it was completely alone and from scratch. He might have the more successful business, the expensive house, the influential network, but Sophie had a grit and determination he could only hope to emulate and learn from.

He'd thought she was beautiful the first time

he'd met her, shivering in the snow, enjoyed her company over the first couple of glasses of wine. He'd been intrigued by her lack of interest in pursuing a relationship with him, a refreshing attitude to his jaded soul, and been taken aback by her horrified response to his family's wealth and influence. There was a grounded realness to Sophie he hadn't come across before. Her experiences could so easily have made her bitter, but instead, although she maintained a guard over her emotions, she was willing and ready to embrace life, to try new things whether it was a small challenge like driving his boat or a huge one like motherhood. He wanted to be with her every step of the way. He just had no idea how to make her believe he meant it.

Marco was quieter than usual. Partly because, like her, he was overwhelmed by the scan bringing the baby to life before their eyes and partly, she suspected, because he was trying his best to show her that he had taken her wishes on board. How long he would manage to consult her before taking any step, from hailing a taxi to opening the door for her, she wasn't sure, but she was touched to see the effort he was making with such sincerity.

The taxi had dropped them off just north of Paddington by a canal filled, to Sophie's delight, with colourful narrowboats. 'They call this area Little Venice,' Marco explained. 'It isn't a patch on the real thing, naturally, but it has a real beauty of its own.'

'I love narrowboats,' Sophie said, staring around her with fascination. 'I've always wanted to live on one and travel from place to place, you know, with pots of herbs and flowers on the roof and maybe a dog.'

'Lovely in summer,' he said doubtfully. 'Probably less romantic in late November when it's been raining for weeks and you can't dry your clothes.'

'It's always sunny in my imagination.' They began walking along the towpath, Sophie peeking in at each boat they passed, squeaking in excitement when she spotted something novel whether it was a cat curled up in the sun or a riotous selection of flowers and vegetables covering the entirety of the boat.

He didn't say that the *palazzo* overlooked a canal on one side, that the terrace and courtyard were big enough to grow all the herbs and flowers she desired, that the heating kept it toasty warm in the colder months and the shuttered windows and thick walls provided shade and coolness in the summer. He didn't need to; she knew it as well as he did.

She knew there were plenty of empty salons just waiting to be put to use, rooms she could line with rails filled with her designs, a drawing board set up by the window, her sewing machine in one corner, a cutting-out table in the other. All that could be hers, she only had to say the word.

But space and money weren't enough. All she wanted, all she'd ever wanted was unconditional love. And for that she'd have gladly lived on a narrowboat through the fiercest of storms.

'There are several cafés on boats, one of which is an Italian deli run by a Venetian man. I can vouch for the quality of both his pasta and his bread. How hungry are you?'

Sophie considered. She could always eat, but was she actually hungry? 'You know, I think if I get a snack to sustain me I would rather walk first, eat afterwards. Is that okay?'

'Of course, it's still early. Why don't we walk up to Regent's Park and decide what to do next from there?'

After a black coffee for Marco and a bottle of sparkling water and a toasted ciabatta filled with mozzarella and tomatoes for Sophie at what was, she conceded, the best Italian café she had been to in London, they headed north towards Maida Vale and Regent's Park. The sun was warm, a gorgeous contrast to the dampness that had characterised most of February and added to the almost holiday atmosphere along the canal side. A family passed them, a baby snug in a sling against its mother's chest, a curly-haired toddler swung high on his father's shoulders. Sophie and Marco paused on the towpath to let them walk by and then stood looking after them as the couple chattered and laughed as they pointed things out to their small son.

Sophie's heart ached. Would she and Marco

ever walk along with their baby in such compatible ease or would it be the polite handovers and lonely nights of a civilised joint custody?

'They look happy,' he said softly as if reading her mind.

'Yes.'

He put a hand on her shoulder and she looked up, surprised, to see a serious expression darkening his eyes. 'Sophie, I just want you to know that I am here for you, whatever you decide to do, however you decide to do it. I know how important your independence is to you. I admire...' he paused, a smile twisting his mouth '...I really admire how hard you've fought for it, fought for everything you've achieved. You should be so proud. I am. I just want you to know that.'

Sophie's heart began to speed up, her throat constricting as she listened to him.

'It's yours, whatever you need, my house in London or the *palazzo* in Venice or somewhere new. For me they are just places, but I want to help you find a home, the right home for you and the baby. If you'll let me. I don't have much else to offer, I realise that now. Strip away my name, strip away my family and there's not much there. I told myself that I didn't need them, that I was enough by myself, yet at the same time I coasted along comfortably on all they brought me. I admit, I didn't think I needed to ask whether you wanted to marry me or not. I'd spent so long running from marriage it didn't occur to me that you might turn me down, want something different for your life. I was an arrogant fool.'

His eyes, still steady on hers, were heavy with sadness and she impulsively lifted a hand to his cheek. 'No, you had good reason to feel that way. I was with you, at that wedding. I saw how people looked at you. I heard what they said. And if I was someone else, if I hadn't been so broken, then maybe I would have said yes. Maybe respect and chemistry would have been enough.'

He shook his head. 'No, you were right. Love is the only basis for marriage. It should be. It's hard enough to succeed at something so huge without starting out short. I didn't think I was the kind of man who could love, but you've taught me differently.'

Her pulse began to hammer so loudly the rest

of the world was drowned out. Was he saying what she thought he was saying?

'I thought of love as selfish, as needy, as constrictive. I thought love meant giving up who you are, what you are. But now I know it means wanting the best for someone else regardless of the cost to you. Tell me what you need from me and I'll do it. Anything. All I want is to be the best father I can be to our child, to make you as proud of me as I am of you.'

All the surety had been wiped away, replaced with a heartfelt expression and the kind of tenderness Sophie hadn't believed could exist in the world, not for her. Scarcely believing, she stared into his face and saw the truth blazing out. He loved her, not because of what she could do, nor because of how she made him feel, but because of who she was.

'Anything?' She couldn't believe her voice was so steady.

'Anything,' he confirmed.

'Then marry me.' She hadn't even known that was what she was going to say, but as soon as she said the words she knew they were right. That they were perfect. 'Marry me three weeks from now in a small ceremony here in London. Just like you wanted, only with the people we love and the people who love us celebrating with us because a wedding should be a celebration, always.'

'It should. I was a fool to think any differently. Sophie, are you sure? You don't have to do this.'

'Surer than I have ever been about anything. I love you, Marco. Saying no to you was the hardest thing I've ever done, but I couldn't be with someone who didn't love me again, not even for the baby.'

'You won't need to,' he vowed. 'Because I love you more than I ever thought possible.' He grinned. 'See how far I've come? My *machismo* is not even slightly dented by your proposal.'

'You did propose to me twice first,' she pointed out. 'Although the first time was more of a fait accompli than an actual proposal.'

Marco caught both her hands in his. 'Not only do I accept your proposal, but I'll make you a promise, here and now, as binding as any wedding vow. We're a team. I'll always remember that. I won't ever try to control you, try to stop you from fulfilling your dreams, from being the person you want to be.'

'That's all I need.' She laced her fingers through his; now she could hold on to him she didn't want to ever let go. 'That's all I ever needed. Your promise and you.'

And as he bent his head to hers to seal their bargain with a kiss Sophie knew she was home at last. London, Venice, a narrowboat cruising the country, wherever Marco was she would be too. She finally had a place of her own.

* * * * *

If you loved this story, make sure you catch the rest of the magical Christmas quartet MAIDS UNDER THE MISTLETOE!

A COUNTESS FOR CHRISTMAS by Christy McKellen

GREEK TYCOON'S MISTLETOE PROPOSAL by Kandy Shepherd

CHRISTMAS IN THE BOSS'S CASTLE by Scarlet Wilson

MILLS & BOON®
Large Print – May 2017

A Deal for the Di Sione Ring
Jennifer Hayward

The Italian's Pregnant Virgin
Maisey Yates

A Dangerous Taste of Passion
Anne Mather

Bought to Carry His Heir
Jane Porter

Married for the Greek's Convenience
Michelle Smart

Bound by His Desert Diamond
Andie Brock

A Child Claimed by Gold
Rachael Thomas

Her New Year Baby Secret
Jessica Gilmore

Slow Dance with the Best Man
Sophie Pembroke

The Prince's Convenient Proposal
Barbara Hannay

The Tycoon's Reluctant Cinderella
Therese Beharrie

MILLS & BOON®
Large Print – June 2017

The Last Di Sione Claims His Prize
Maisey Yates

Bought to Wear the Billionaire's Ring
Cathy Williams

The Desert King's Blackmailed Bride
Lynne Graham

Bride by Royal Decree
Caitlin Crews

The Consequence of His Vengeance
Jennie Lucas

The Sheikh's Secret Son
Maggie Cox

Acquired by Her Greek Boss
Chantelle Shaw

The Sheikh's Convenient Princess
Liz Fielding

The Unforgettable Spanish Tycoon
Christy McKellen

The Billionaire of Coral Bay
Nikki Logan

Her First-Date Honeymoon
Katrina Cudmore

MILLS & BOON®

Why shop at millsandboon.co.uk?

Each year, thousands of romance readers find their perfect read at millsandboon.co.uk. That's because we're passionate about bringing you the very best romantic fiction. Here are some of the advantages of shopping at www.millsandboon.co.uk:

* **Get new books first**—you'll be able to buy your favourite books one month before they hit the shops

* **Get exclusive discounts**—you'll also be able to buy our specially created monthly collections, with up to 50% off the RRP

* **Find your favourite authors**—latest news, interviews and new releases for all your favourite authors and series on our website, plus ideas for what to try next

* **Join in**—once you've bought your favourite books, don't forget to register with us to rate, review and join in the discussions

Visit **www.millsandboon.co.uk**
for all this and more today!